Mysterious Creatures of Britain

JG Montgomery

First published in 2025 by Blossom Spring Publishing
Mysterious Creatures of Britain
Copyright © 2025 JG Montgomery
ISBN 978-1-917938-00-6
E: admin@blossomspringpublishing.com
W: www.blossomspringpublishing.com

Introduction

Mysterious Creatures of Britain

There are marten cats and badgers and foxes in the
Enchanted Woods but there are of a certainty, mightier
creatures, and the lake hides what neither line nor
net can take.

William Butler Yeats *(The Celtic Twilight)*

In 2014, I wrote a book titled *WYRD—A journey into the
beliefs and philosophies of the known and unknown,*
which was published by CFZ Publications in Devon. In it,
I explored a range of cryptozoological, supernatural and
mythological creatures and events, including the legendary
Bunyip, real dragons, and apparent sea monsters, as well as
vampires, witches, fairies, alien big cats, Bigfoot, ghosts, and
other paranormal or cryptozoological creatures. I attempted
to analyse the evidence and reports of these strange creatures
and phenomena and offering a rational explanation where
one existed or, when it didn't, simply leaving it open.

Having said this, can we really rationally explain all
these bizarre encounters or has the hustle and bustle of
modern-day living killed the romantic ideals of the old
ways and old beliefs? Do we now live in a world that is
too busy for fantastic stories and unbelievable beings?
And have we, through our detachment, killed off these
creatures? In other words, do we, as adults, allow
pragmatism to kill the childish instincts within us—that
belief that something amazing could be just around the
corner, whether it be something that is completely and

utterly impossible, like, for instance, Bigfoot or the Loch Ness Monster, or something as simple as a crab in an ocean pool?

Is it possible that these creatures could actually exist? Eyewitness reports, although sometimes unreliable, seem to suggest that, yes, these strange creatures could possibly exist. After all, how can so many people report so many sightings of the Loch Ness Monster, or Bigfoot, or alien big cats? Could they all be mistaken? Is it simply a case of mass hysteria or misidentification? Let us look at it in another way: even if ten percent of the sighting of strange creatures or phenomena were correct, then we are looking at a world that contains much that we do not understand.

A close colleague of mine, Tim the Yowieman, is a self-described cryptonaturalist. Together, we have examined numerous ghost stories, as well as reports of extraordinary animals, and he is adamant that he witnessed a Yowie—the Australian equivalent of Bigfoot—while bushwalking in the rugged bushlands to the southwest of Canberra. Equally, I have no doubt that I saw a large black panther slinking across a field on the outskirts of the same city back in the late 1990s. Maybe both of us misinterpreted what we saw? Maybe Tim saw nothing more than a large man in a dark jacket? Maybe I saw a normal house cat?

And yet I know what I saw, as does Tim. We have not misinterpreted the facts. Indeed, over time, I have often questioned myself as to what it was that I saw that day. If anything, I now have a stronger conviction that what I saw was indeed a large black panther-like creature, and this leads me to think, what of the hundreds of other sightings of strange, anomalous creatures?

For instance, in Tasmania people repeatedly report sightings of the Tasmanian tiger, *Thylacinus cynocephalus*, even though it was declared extinct by the International Union for Conservation of Nature in 1982 and by the Tasmanian government in 1986. Is it possible, in such a wilderness like Tasmania, that these creatures could still exist? And the same could be said for other, less well-known zoological specimens, remembering that the coelacanth, a living fossil, was only discovered half a century ago. Indeed, the mountain gorilla, something familiar to everyone these days, was only discovered a century or so ago.

Along the same lines, just recently explorers in Indonesia came across an extinct volcano crater that was filled with new and wonderful creatures, including a giant rat as big as a small dog. As such it would be a brave person to bet against the possibility that some of the creatures mentioned in this book could exist.

Having said this, we are not looking through the wilds of Tasmania or Indonesia but Great Britain, a place where humans have lived for thousands upon thousands of years and a land where the countryside has been irrevocably changed by this human inhabitancy. It is not, by any stretch of the imagination, the wilds of deepest darkest Africa or even the desolate outback of Australia, let alone the North American wilderness. Surely such a place could not hold such strange creatures?

In *WYRD* I not only looked at strange and out-of-place animals but also supernatural creatures, such as vampires.

And in doing so I found that, although these days vampires seem fairly commonplace in literature, film and television, there is a strong historic record of these creatures. Whether or not they are blood-sucking undead creatures is debatable, but once again, history and culture show us that, if they do not exist in reality, they certainly exist in folklore and beliefs. And these beliefs always have a basis in fact somewhere, as we shall see in later chapters.

I also looked at fairies, imps and other assorted little folk which, again, we see throughout history and who are deeply embedded in culture, so much so that these creatures are believed to exist. And, as we will discover, fairies and the like were once thought of as being real, as real as a bear, otter, or any other animal. And, as such, we must ask: why? Is it possible, however unbelievable that these creatures existed? Do the little people appear now and then to select humans for some unknown reason? Once again, how can so many people be so wrong?

We shall also touch upon black dogs and mermaids. Although both may seem far from the realms of possibility, we again find that they feature heavily in culture and half-remembered folklore. Indeed, the black dog legend still runs strong in many parts of the United Kingdom.

We can just about discount mermaids, given that old-time sailors most probably misinterpreted what they saw. And yet, once again, we have an amazing number of accounts of these seaborne creatures, which leads us to ask: could it be possible? One would think not. However, this is not to say that other strange creatures don't exist in the seas, lakes and oceans; thus, we found ourselves dealing with other giants—this time in the form of lake monsters, modern-day dinosaurs, and other strange creatures. And, of all lake monsters, we can agree that the Loch Ness Monster is probably the most well-known.

But being well known is not a criterion for being real. And yet the Loch Ness Monster, reportedly seen by so many people over such a long time, is one creature that we can definitely say *might* exist. Indeed, although photos of the beast have been inconclusive—in some cases obviously faked—the reports are fascinating. Could some sort of undiscovered dinosaur-like creature exist in the loch? Is the fantastic Rines photograph that of the monster's fin, or is it just a random piece of driftwood that happens to look something like a fin? Of course, in saying this, one must remember that lake monsters are not the sole domain of Scotland, given that reports of them exist all over the world. These include such serpent-like creatures like Champ, Morag, Ogopogo, and many more. Is it a coincidence that these lake monsters generally seem to have the same characteristics?

Like the Tasmanian Tiger and the Tasmanian wilderness, could Loch Ness be hiding one of the most important zoological discoveries of all time? Ridiculous as it may seem, the humble old coelacanth has shown us that notions of present-day dinosaurs may not be all that far-fetched.

But if we seem to encounter aquatic monsters in lakes, rivers and swamps, then what of the sea, that vast, largely unexplored part of the world that hides almost everything that lives in it? Could there be unknown species lurking in its depths? If one is to believe the reports, then one would have to say *yes*; one could also suggest that the oceans and seas of this globe would be the one place where strange and monstrous creatures could live without ever being detected.

But, as weird as these may be, they pale in comparison to the strange stories of the Cornish Owlman and other extraordinary, bipedal, hairy, human-like figures that haunt remote and scarcely populated forests. While these creatures (such as Bigfoot, the Yeti, or the Yowie of Australian legend) may not be as prevalent in the British Isles, there are numerous reports that suggest that something may be out there.

Is it possible that these creatures are one and the same, or maybe related to each other in some way, having been separated hundreds of thousands of years ago with the breakup of continents? Could the Yeti simply be an alpine version of the Bigfoot, much like the polar bear and grizzly bear are obvious cousins? And, when we think about it, we really only just missed the Neanderthals by a few tens of thousands of years—a mere blip in Earth's timeline. In fact, that figure could possibly be much less; we just haven't yet found the evidence.

But these are questions that, at present, we cannot answer: the evidence is neither forthcoming nor available. Will the coming years change this? Will we find one day that Bigfoot is recognised as a form of large ape, much like the gorilla, which—we must remember—was only discovered a little over a century ago? Surely this is not beyond the realms of possibility, given that the coelacanth, a true living fossil, was only recently discovered in the seas off Madagascar?

When we are talking about mysterious creatures, that may or may not exist, we need to remember that there must still be thousands, if not tens of thousands, of yet-to-be-discovered creatures in remote and isolated pockets of the world. Indeed, to think otherwise would be to be imprudent in the extreme. In fact, many unknown creatures—animals, fish, insects, birds—may not be that unknown to locals. It may be that, like thylacine reports from Papua New Guinea, no one has actually bothered to report them.

And like the famed Tasmanian tiger, reports of alien big cats, whether they be in Australia or England, seem to indicate that it is highly possible that they exist. Indeed, one could almost say that it is likely. Numerous witnesses have reported these beasts and, although sceptics will point out that what they are seeing is nothing more than a dog or a very large and feral cat, people generally know and understand what a panther is and what it looks like. I have no doubt that what I saw that day at Birrigai, on the outskirts of Canberra, was a panther. There was simply no other explanation. It was not a dog, or a feral pig, or a kangaroo with an injured leg—it was a panther. Maybe one day soon an unfortunate beast will wander onto a road and be hit by a car. And, although a sad ending for the big cat, it will at least affirm the suspicions of many that these creatures *do* exist in the desolate, windswept moors of southwestern England.

When one talks about mysteries, both creatures and phenomena, we must remember that only a few millennia ago almost *everything* was a mystery: the sun rising in the morning, the moon and stars at night. Some things were terrifying; others were familiar—but all were a mystery, as man at that time did not have the understanding to explain what he was seeing or experiencing. And maybe this is why religions began to flourish, as a way to explain a world that made very little sense.

These days, the range of people interested in such mysteries spans from the benign onlooker to the interested scientists, and slightly deranged self-titled researchers who add very little to the argument. An example of this is the current discussion taking place in the Bigfoot/Sasquatch world, where some believe that the creature is nothing more than a large undiscovered ape or remnant Neanderthal, while others passionately argue that the creature is somewhat paranormal and exists within a different dimension, with the ability to transfer between our world and theirs with ease. How else do they stay hidden or disappear so fast, they argue? Well, says the other camp, it is a very skilful hider and can run fast. Whatever the case, the two will never meet—which is what makes mysteries interesting. After all, if we *did* know the answer then it would no longer be a mystery and therefore would not hold the allure that it once did.

On the other hand, we have mysteries such as sea serpents, which most zoologists would admit could exist. Indeed, the prospect of large unidentified sea creatures roaming the depths is probably not far-fetched in any way, and maybe it is only a matter of time before we see evidence of this. Of course, extraordinary claims will always need extraordinarily high standards of verification and validation, but a dead plesiosaur lying on a deserted beach on the coast of the United States, or some other country, will certainly aid that verification.

Of course, one does not have to believe anything that I have discussed in this book; on the other hand, let's hope it opens up discussion and encourages a little more interest in these topics. After all, if man had never attempted to discover the reason for strange things, we would not be where we are now. And, while I am not suggesting that all these incredible creatures exist, I am also not discounting the possibility, however remote, that they *could* exist.

If this book does anything, apart from maybe awakening the imagination or interest of a few inquisitive minds, it is to show that there is a lot in this world than we know little about, and indeed, there is much more in this world that we simply do not know anything about.

And, as William Shakespeare once wrote:

There are more things in heaven and earth, Horatio,
Than are dreamt of in your philosophy.

JG Montgomery
(Canberra 2024)

Chapter One

Mermaids and Other Creatures of the Sea

Mermaid stories have been around for centuries and are a large part of British seafaring lore. This is especially true for the coastal regions of the south-west, including Cornwall, where the sighting of a mermaid is thought to be, like a black dog, a portent of doom—an omen foretelling storms, rough seas, and even death.

Descriptions of mermaids are remarkably similar, not only in the British Isles, but worldwide. Generally, their upper body is that of a beautiful, lithe young woman with long hair, and their lower body is that of a fish. Often, they are to be found sitting on a rock just offshore, combing their hair and singing, or admiring their beauty in a handheld mirror.

Their singing is said to be so beautiful that, like the alluring sirens of classical times, it can lure sailors to their death—to be drowned, dashed on the rocks, or dragged into the depths and eaten. Indeed, Mermaid's Rock, near Lamorna in Cornwall, is just one place where a mermaid is said to sit and sing, luring fishermen to their deaths. Another remarkable folk tale tells of the mermaid of Zennor, a small village not far from St Ives in Cornwall, where, in the church, carved on the end of one of the wooden pews, is the figure of a mermaid holding a mirror in one hand and a comb in the other.

The legend of the mermaid of Zennor describes how, many years ago, a well-dressed and very beautiful woman attended a ceremony at the local church. No one knew her or where she was from but all were impressed by her beauty and her lovely singing voice. As such, she soon caught the eye of one of the locals, Mathew Trewella, a handsome young man who was blessed with an excellent singing voice. After one Sunday service, Trewella decided to follow the mysterious woman as she walked away towards the cliffs. He was never seen again.

Many years passed, and the memory of Trewella and his unexplained disappearance faded. That is, until one morning when a ship cast anchor off Pendower Cove, near Zennor, and the captain of the ship, who was sitting on deck, heard a lovely voice calling him from the sea. Looking over the side into the clear waters, he saw a beautiful mermaid with long blonde hair.

From the water, the mermaid asked the incredulous captain if he would raise the anchor as it was resting upon the doorway of her house, and she wanted to get back to her husband, Mathew, and her children. She then told him that the beautiful stranger from the church, all those years ago, was in fact a mermaid called Morveren, one of the daughters of Llyr, Celtic god of the sea.

The captain, fearing that the mermaid would bring bad luck to him and his ship, weighed anchor and headed for deeper water. Later, however, he returned and, upon docking, went into Zennor and told the townsfolk of the fate of Mathew Trewella. To commemorate this event, and to serve as a warning to other men, a mermaid was carved into a pew at the local church.

Another version of the story tells how Morveren was drawn to the church by Trewella's beautiful singing and, so she could hear him more clearly, she would dress as a human and listen at the back of the church. Every night, at evensong, the mermaid would come to hear him. One night, as Trewella sang a particularly lovely verse, Morveren let out a sigh that was heard by no one except Trewella.

Trewella then turned and looked at the mermaid, whose veil slipped from her head, revealing wet, gleaming hair. In an instant, Trewella was love-struck. However, Morveren fled back to the sea, fearing that she would be recognised as a mermaid. Trewella and some of the locals followed her and, in her panic, she tripped. At that moment, Trewella noticed that she did not have legs, but the tail of a fish.

Morveren told Trewella that she could not stay: she was a creature of the sea and had to go back to where she belonged. Trewella replied, telling the mermaid that if *she* belonged in the sea, then so did *he*. He then picked her up and carried her to the sea, where the two disappeared beneath the waves.

It was said that when Trewella sang soft and high the day would be fair, and when he sang deep and low then the seas would be rough. From his songs, the fishermen of Zennor knew when it was safe to put to sea and when it was wise to remain at anchor in the harbour.

But Zennor isn't the only place where mermaids are said to exist. In 1830, some locals were harvesting seaweed at Sgeir na Duchadh on the Outer Hebridean island of Benbecula, when a woman saw a small human-like creature splashing in the sea only a few feet away. She called her friends, and soon a group of people watched the odd creature as it swam about and performed somersaults. Some of the men tried to wade out to the 'animal', but it started to swim away. Frightened, some boys threw stones at the creature and one struck it—apparently causing a fatal blow, because a few days later its dead body washed ashore two miles away.

Alexander Carmichael wrote in his encyclopædia, *Carmina Gadelica*: "The upper portion of the creature was about the size of a well-fed child of three or four years of age, with an abnormally developed breast." He added: "The hair was long, dark, and glossy, while the skin was white, soft, and tender. The lower part of the body was like a salmon, but without scales."

Apparently, crowds of people—some from long distances—came to see the mermaid, and all were unanimous in the opinion that what they had seen was indeed a mermaid. Mr Duncan Shaw, baron-bailie and sheriff of the district, ordered a coffin and shroud to be made for the mermaid, and when this was completed, the body was buried a short distance above the shore, where it was found. Attempts to locate the grave, however, have so far been unsuccessful.

Mermaids, it is said, possess the ability to grant the gift of magical powers to people, although there is a high price to pay for those on whom the gift has been bestowed. In the story of Lutey and the Mermaid, a Cornish fisherman found a stranded mermaid on the shore while he was beachcombing and helped her back to the sea. As a result, she offered him three wishes. He chose the power to break spells, the power to compel spirits for the good of others, and that these powers pass down his family line.

Thankful for being saved, the mermaid granted the fisherman his wishes but, as he was about to lower her into the sea, she grabbed at him and tried to pull him into the water. The fisherman panicked but managed to get hold of a fishing knife, which he brandished at the mermaid. Repelled by the blade made of iron, as is traditional for supernatural and ghostly creatures, the mermaid released her hold and the fisherman escaped a watery death. However, after nine years of using his gifts, the mermaid returned for him, and he was compelled to follow her to his death in the depths. Thereafter, every nine years one of his descendants was said to be lost at sea.

Although most folk tales tell of sea-dwelling mermaids, it appears that they are not completely confined to the briny depths, as there are numerous examples of mermaids haunting rivers and deep pools. Mermaids Pool, below Kinder Downfall in Derbyshire, is one such location. The mermaid at this location appears only on a specific date and is said to possess a treacherous nature. Black Mere, near Leek in Staffordshire, is also thought to be inhabited by a mermaid, which leads us to speculate that the term *mermaid* can be used to describe quite a variety of supernatural, human-like water creatures.

Indeed, if one were to look at the phenomena of

mermaids in a logical light, one could say that the Lady of the Lake from Arthurian legend was quite possibly a freshwater mermaid, remembering that she was not only the foster mother of Sir Lancelot (and raised him beneath the murky waters of the lake), but also presented the sword Excalibur to Arthur.

Known variously as Nimue, Viviane, Elaine, Niniane, Nivian, Nyneve—as well as other variations of these names—she initially met Merlin, Arthur's trusted magician, at the fountain of Barenton in Brittany. Enchanted, the young Merlin fell deeply in love with her, agreeing to teach her all his magical powers. Over time, however, she became so powerful that her magical skills were greater than those of Merlin himself, and she imprisoned him in a glass tower while replacing him at the King's side.

The Lady of the Lake was eventually obliged to reclaim her sword after Arthur was fatally wounded at the Battle of Camlann, and Sir Bedivere hurled the sword back into misty waters. She was later one of the queens who escorted the wounded and dying Arthur to the mystic isle of Avalon.

Of course, as with most Arthurian stories, there is another angle, and one could suggest that, because the Lady of the Lake's place as Merlin's student and lover was largely overtaken by Morgan le Fay, the two were actually the same person. Indeed, Morgan le Fay incidentally means 'water-nymph'. Having said this, both of them appear as queens who escorted Arthur to Avalon.

As well as appearing to be able to grant wishes,

mermaids are also said to be able to intermarry with humans, as we have already seen in the case of Mathew Trewella. Unsurprisingly, it is said that the children of these liaisons are somewhat magical themselves; indeed, they possess some of the powers of fairies, which leads us to ponder whether fairies are, in fact, fairies, or the offspring of humans and mermaids? And, if the latter, then are all fairies and assorted 'little folk'—goblins, brownies, Knockers, piskies and the like—the offspring of mermaids and humans?

Of course, this argument seems scarcely believable, yet it does illustrate how folklore does not have to be logical in its views, ideals and conclusions. And, by not being a slave to logic, folklore allows itself to open up to worlds that cannot possibly exist—or, if they do, are too fantastic for us to imagine. And herein lies the allure of this world, a world where almost anything can happen.

As strange as it may seem, mermaids (or, at least, strange water creatures) have been regularly reported in the British Isles. In July 1826, on the cliffs near Aberystwyth, twelve people watched as a beautiful, pale woman, with what appeared to be a black tail, washed herself in the sea. And in 1810, on the Isle of Man, three men from Douglas found two merchildren on the rocks: one was already dead, but they saved the second child and took it into town. The creature was described as around two feet high and brown in colour, although the scales around its tail were slightly violet, and the hair on its head light green. Whatever happened to it is not known, or at least, is not recorded.

At Campbeltown, in October 1811, a mermaid was watched by a farmer for two hours. Apparently, it had a pale upper body and a reddish-grey tail covered in hair. Its face was human, with deep-set eyes and short neck. The creature combed the hair on its head with what looked like short, stubby arms, before diving into the water and washing its torso.

As recently as 1872, a merman was seen off the coast of Castlemartin by a Mr Henry Reynolds, who initially believed he was looking at a pale-skinned teenager before noticing its brown tail that waved about. He also noted that, while the body and arms looked human, the arms and hands appeared too short and thick, and the creature's nose was long and sharp. Reynolds went to find other witnesses, but by the time he returned the creature had gone.

In Deerness in the Orkneys, there have been many reported sightings of mermaids. Around 1890, over a couple of summer periods, the Deerness mermaid used to show herself to visitors to Newark Bay, with apparently little to no fear of being spotted. And, although there are no real details given about her appearance, as she swam some distance from the shore to stay safe, she was nonetheless watched by literally hundreds of eyewitnesses.

Interestingly, she was not described as being like the classical mermaid of legend, in that she was reportedly "seven feet in length and had a dark black head and neck upon its shoulders. The skin of its torso was a deep pale white colour and it had long arms that it used to swim about in a waving motion. It also rather creepily slid up and down rocks under the water—using them to protrude and then disappear back into the water again. It was as if she was waving through the water in a sort of dance motion."

And so, mermaid and merman sightings may not be as unusual as one may think. While many sightings can be attributed to manatees and other unidentified sea creatures, not all cases can be dismissed outright as a case of mistaken identity, which leads us to ask: if mermaids and mermen are *not* a case of misinterpretation, then what on earth are they? And how do they fit in with our pragmatic and ordered world? Is it possible that, like fairies, goblins, elves and the like, they make up some strange and unseen part of our world? A world that exists in another dimension, a world that we simply cannot see for reasons unknown?

Water deities have always been respected in Celtic societies as they were believed to be able to control the essence of life itself. The natural and fluid movements of springs, rivers and lakes clearly showed the supernatural powers of the goddesses who lived in the water and, as such, offerings— especially of weapons and other valuables—at such aquatic features were commonplace. Indeed, archaeological sites today still give up broken swords, boot buckles, coins, and other items that reinforce how strong the belief in these water creatures was.

Another water-dwelling creature of mythology, the selkie, also a shape-shifting creature found in Irish and Scottish folklore, is a seal which can shed its skin. In myth, the selkie can become human by removing its seal skin and can return to being a seal by simply putting it back on again. Folklore surrounding selkies is generally composed of romantic tragedies in which the human does not know that their lover is a selkie and wakes to find them gone.

It has been said that children born as a result of a union between a mortal person and selkie were relatively common and, until fairly recently, some Orcadian families still claimed descent from the selkie folk. One supposedly true story, documented by Walter Traill Dennison, an Orcadian folklorist who died in 1894, tells of how the children of one North Isles family were all born with webbed feet and fingers: the midwife present at the birth clipped the webs with shears, "and many a clipping Ursilla clipped, to keep the fins from growing again; and the fins, not being able to grow in their natural way, grew into a horny crust on the palms of the hands and soles of the feet. And this horny substance can be seen in many of Ursilla's descendants to this day." Dennison also stated that, "Whatever may be thought of this tale, its last sentence is quite true."

Apparently, a selkie can only make contact with one particular human for a short amount of time before they must return to the sea, which is very similar to the mermaid of myths. Given this, it appears that the mythical selkie and the mermaid are both folklore tales that come from the same source, whatever that source may be. Unlike the kelpie and assorted water horses, the selkie appears not to be dangerous in any way.

Having said that, an old mermaid tale from Dunkettle in County Cork tells of a great eel that lived in a graveyard and terrorised the town, eating sheep and cattle until one morning a man tending a graveyard managed to sever its tail. The enraged creature attacked but the man managed to escape, although suffering fatal wounds. As a consequence of his wounds, the man died; one of the headstones in the graveyard is said to be decorated with an eel and a hook.

And so, although the last report is not exactly that of a mermaid, we find that reports of large unidentified water creatures in British lakes and lochs have been around for centuries, something we shall explore in depth in a further chapter. However, at this stage we shall remain with mysterious creatures of the oceans and seas, which, of course, should involve those infamous denizens of the deep: sea monsters.

Contrary to popular belief, the sailors of ancient times did not think, like Erik and his crew in the film *Erik the Viking,* that they would sail off the edge of the earth. They were, however, apprehensive about what they would find on their travels, given mistakes about marine life, ranging from inaccurate assumptions about the behaviour of known species to fanciful depictions of animals that might exist. Indeed, one only need look at maritime charts from the sixteenth century to see that sea monsters were perceived to be a real threat.

Over the years, the seas and oceans have captivated humans. We have plundered its bountiful harvest, explored its endless open kilometres, painted its beauty, and died in its icy depths. We have fought wars over it and on it, discovered its splendour and its terrifying destruction, and all the while remained beguiled by its romantic intrigue and its limitless unknown secrets. And more importantly, we still know little about its depths and what creatures it holds.

As with Loch Ness and other landlocked bodies of water, the oceans of our planet, unsurprisingly, hold their own extraordinary and wonderful creatures: some known, some not, and others imagined or suspected. And, like the denizens of lochs and lakes, these creatures also appear to be out of time—that is, they appear to be dinosaurs or remnants of prehistoric creatures that occasionally reveal themselves to solitary ship lookouts or wash up on isolated beaches, to the bemused of onlookers and scientists.

Sightings of such sea serpents have been reported for hundreds, if not thousands, of years and continue to the present. This was amply illustrated by the Zuiyo-maru carcass dragged aboard a Japanese trawler in April 1977 which, although in the end was most likely to be the rotting carcass of a basking shark, nevertheless stoked imagination and speculation that sea monsters still could conceivably exist in the vast depths of the oceans. Although there have been an estimated 1,200 or more sightings of sea monsters in various guises, it is believed that the sightings can be best explained as being known animals such as oarfish and various whales. That said, some cryptozoologists have suggested that the sea serpents are relict plesiosaurs, mosasaurs or other Mesozoic marine reptiles—an idea often associated with lake monsters.

Descriptions of sea serpents appear to have a number of things in common. However, there also appears to be enough variety to suggest that there could be numerous different species. Some have been described in a variety of colours such as black, brown, grey and green, and range in size from twenty feet to hundreds of feet in length. They are generally reported to move in an undulating motion and have, like the Loch Ness Monster, a series of humps visible above the water. They generally have a split tail, like a whale, and may have one or more pairs of flippers along their length. Sometimes they have been described as having armoured segments like a millipede, large plates or scales like a fish, or a smooth rubbery skin like a mammal such as a whale or seal.

And although these creatures seem to regularly appear all over the world, from Europe to Australia and the Americas, they also appear in the British Isles. In Stronsay, one of the Orkney Islands, a farmer by the name of George Sherar found a huge but unknown creature washed ashore, just below the high tide mark. He measured it at fifty-five feet long, with a fifteen-foot neck. It had a small head and a long mane running along the length of its body. Bizarrely, it had three pairs of legs, with each foot having five or six toes. He salvaged some vertebrae and the skull, and the creature became known as the Stronsay Beast.

An eminent naturalist, Sir Everard Home, an expert on the basking shark (the world's second-largest shark species), compared Sherar's specimen with those of a basking shark and found that they matched very closely, indicating that the creature was probably a basking shark that had rotted away whilst on the beach. Still, it should be noted that the largest basking shark ever caught was in 1851 in Canada and, at forty feet in length, was still fifteen feet shorter than the Stronsay Beast.

Dr Yvonne Simpson, a geneticist who has been studying the remains since 2001, and who believed newly recovered bone fragments may finally help solve the mystery regarding the creature's identity, suggested to *The Telegraph* in 2008 that well-preserved bone fragments—given to her by a private collector—may reveal the DNA of the creature.

Dr Simpson, who works in archaeogenetics—the analysis of DNA recovered from archaeological remains—stated that the new DNA sequences could make identification possible for the first time. However, as a cautionary note, she added that, "At fifty-five feet long this would be an unusually big basking shark, and it's far more likely to belong to another member of the shark family."

Exceptionally large basking shark or not, the Orkneys have a long tradition of sea monsters including the nuckelavee, a hybrid, sea-living creature described as having the features of both a mighty horse and its rider. The rider was legless and appeared to grow straight out of the horse's back. Its head was ten times the size of a normal human head, with a very wide mouth that jutted out like a pig's snout, and a single red eye that blazed with flame. It was both hairless and skinless, and its breath was toxic.

Whereas the previous report reads more like mythology than an actual sea monster report, the following accounts are more compelling.

In the 1850s on the Island of Hoy, also in the Orkneys, a young boy called Alec Groundwater reported that he was sitting on some rocks when he was attacked by a sea monster with what appeared to be a horse's mane. Reportedly, it tried to bite his legs and drag him into the water but was unsuccessful. Leaping back from its teeth, the boy remained on the rock, watching in terror as the sea creature made a number of attempts to reach him. Eventually it "rose once more to shake its head and mane till the water cascaded from it on all sides, then disappeared".

Understandably, the boy was terrified and only managed to give a vague description of the beast. He described it as having a flat head, a long mane (similar to that of a horse), and a wide mouth which housed wicked-looking teeth or tusks. Interestingly, many years later, in the same area, it was also reported that a diver who was investigating the wreck of a sunken German ship suddenly realised that he was standing on the back of a large sea monster that had made its home in the wreck.

In November 1905, two men fishing off Shapinsay claimed they had encountered a sea creature, which they described as having a body like a horse and "covered with a scaly surface and spotted".

The *Orcadian* of 11 November 1905 described the encounter thus: "The sea serpent has again made its appearance, and at present it is enjoying itself in the boisterous waters of the String, with a tendency to sun itself near Shapinsay, quite close to the rocks under Balfour Castle. Last Saturday two fishermen were working their creels off the 'Douch' when the monster suddenly raised itself out of the water at the side of their boat. The visit was so sudden and unexpected that the men cannot give a very particular description of the monster. Of one thing they are certain, however, and that is that the serpent had an awe-inspiring appearance, and was quite different from anything they had ever seen before.

"The body is described as massive as that of horse, covered with a scaly surface, and spotted. It was the eyes of the monster, however, that attracted most attention. These are said to have been as large as a bowl, and had a most fascinating attraction for the beholder.

"After gazing at the occupants of the boat for a second or two the uncanny visitant, gradually sank out of view, much to the relief of the fishermen. The same men, when fishing near the same place on Wednesday last, had another glimpse of the sea serpent…"

Of course, such a report caused quite a sensation, with some suggesting that the creature was simply an overly large seal while others leaned towards the sea serpent proposition. Whatever the case, something large appeared that day to experienced, hardened fishermen who were in no doubt as to what they saw.

Likewise, in August 1919, five men were fishing off Brims, a village at the southern tip of the island of Hoy, when a creature came to within thirty yards of their boat and was described as having a neck as thick as an elephant's foreleg, sticking about five to six feet out of the water. Speaking to *The Orcadian* newspaper at the time, one man said: "The neck I should say stuck about five to six feet, possibly more, out of the water. My friends thought it would weigh two or three tonnes, some thinking four to six. If the neck stretched, say, to eight feet, the neck and body would be eighteen to twenty feet long."

But these are not the only reports of strange seagoing creatures in the Orkneys: in August 1936, Henry Stout, who lived at Leagar, Outertown, visited the offices of *The Orcadian* and recalled how he and his son had been working in a field when they noticed an object of considerable size less than a mile from the shore, moving at a considerable speed. As the creature got nearer to the shore, they spotted four sail-like fins, the ones in front about five feet high and four feet long, with smaller fins visible along the rest of the body and situated at ten-foot intervals. Stout estimated that the creature must have been at least forty feet long, and the two watched it for more than half an hour before it dived below the surface and disappeared.

Stout commented that he had "lived at Leagar, Outertown, for forty years, and [was] familiar with all the aspects of the sea in that area. [He had] formerly engaged in cod fishing and [was] well acquainted with the habits of basking sharks, porpoises, flights of birds, and whales. This object [they] watched was none of these."

In the same month, James Marwick, writing for *The Orcadian* reported an anonymous monster sighting from Rousay, quoting: "It was in the sea, about two hundred yards off the shore, straight opposite Nethermill, Sourin.

Two friends, along with my brother, saw it also. My brother, a friend and I first had a good look with the spyglass at it. All we could see was a big head, with long ears and very long neck. We were not satisfied with that so my brother and I launched a boat and went off to get a better look. As we came near, it turned round, head-on towards us about twelve or fourteen feet away. This is what we saw: a big round head with small black eyes, big drooping ears, long tapered neck, and a very heavy-looking thick body, altogether about nine or ten feet long; slate-grey in colour and smooth-skinned like a porpoise."

Then, in August 1937, Mr John R. Brown, an occasional lighthouse keeper on the Pentland Skerries, sighted another enormous sea creature. His sighting was duly reported in the local newspaper: "I never believed much in monsters myself but I saw something today resembling nothing I have ever seen before. It was about noon, when we were working down at the landing at the east end, that on chancing to look out to sea I noticed the sea breaking white as if on a submerged rock. As I knew there were no rocks on that particular spot, I watched for a little, and presently a great object rose up out of the water, anything from twenty to thirty feet, and at an angle of forty-five degrees. It was round-shaped and there appeared to be a head on it, but as it was about half a mile from the shore, I could not be sure."

Brown later stressed his sighting was definitely not a killer whale, something he was quite familiar with.

A few weeks prior to Brown's sighting, workmen on the Fair Isle reported seeing an extremely large "monster" approach them. As a colleague was in the water, the men were about to issue a warning signal when the creature veered off and disappeared beneath the waves, obviously uninterested in the man in the water. The workmen reported that the creature reappeared sometime later and remained some distance from the shore, swimming around in the sea throughout the afternoon.

Again, one could be forgiven for thinking that the men had simply seen a large seal, or possibly a whale, and yet, as in previous monster encounters in the area, they were convinced that what they saw was not an animal they were familiar with. They were, like other witnesses, adamant that they had seen a so-called sea monster. And given the history of sea serpent sightings in the Orkney area, it is hard not to side with this view.

Whatever the case, if the Stronsay Beast or other sea monsters seen in the Orkneys were simply cases of misidentification, then what can one make of Morgawr, a huge plesiosaur-like beast, believed to haunt the sea near Falmouth Bay, Cornwall?

First sighted in 1906, the proof of its existence depends, like most sea and lake monsters, completely on eyewitness accounts and a few low-quality but otherwise impressive photographs. Having said this, the eyewitness accounts for such a beast present quite a strong case for the existence of *something* in the region.

As recently as September 1975, two witnesses claim to have seen a humped figure with stumpy horns and bristles on its back off Pendennis Point. The witnesses even stated that it had a large Conger eel in its mouth, which pretty much discounts the possibility that it was, in fact, a giant eel of some description.

Six months later, in February 1976, a woman known only as 'Mary F' sent two photographs to the *Falmouth Packet*, a local newspaper. These photos seemingly showed a large unidentified creature lolling on the water's surface at Rosemullion Head. The woman added: "It looked like an elephant waving its trunk, but the trunk was a long neck with a small head at the end, like a snake's head. It had humps on its back which moved in a funny way." She also said: "The animal frightened me. I would not like to see it any closer. I do not like the way it moved when swimming."

Sadly, neither 'Mary F' nor the negatives have ever been traced and, although the photographs have been examined and declared as most probably genuine, there will always be doubt as to their authenticity due to the woman's wish to remain anonymous. And so, whether the photos are a superb fake or genuine sea monster will never be known.

In fact, 1976 seemed to be a good year for monster spotting in Cornwall: in July, at Lizard Point, fishermen John Cock and George Vinnicombe claimed to have seen a creature whose neck reared four feet up in the water and was an estimated length of twenty-two feet. Then, in November, at Parson's Beach, Mawnan, a Mr Tony Shiels claimed to photograph the creature lying low in the water, complete with little stumpy horns on its head, although this sighting only estimated the creature's length as at fifteen feet. Interestingly, Cornwall in 1976 was the site of another extremely bizarre paranormal occurrence: the sighting of a so-called Owlman, which we shall examine in greater detail later in this book.

In August 1985, at Gerran's Bay—also in Cornwall—Christopher and Susan Waldron of Gloucestershire reported seeing a strange creature whilst on holiday. Mrs Waldron stated that she was watching her husband swimming in the sea when she noticed a large silhouette under the surface behind him. The shape was described to be that of a large, long-necked creature. Even more frightening, in 1987 at Devil's Point off Plymouth, an experienced diver reported seeing a dog-like head on a neck rising a metre out of the sea. However, the area is noted as a spot frequented by Conger eels, although this sighting would suggest an eel of immense size—indeed, much larger than any ever recorded.

In 2007 I was lucky enough, on one of my regular English sojourns, to spend some time in Cornwall and the West Country. While ostensibly researching ghosts and the supernatural for another book, I also managed to do some sightseeing along the coastline where the legendary Morgawr was reputed to live.

And so, on a cool but sunny morning, I boarded a tiny blue-hulled fishing boat in the tiny Cornish coastal town of Polperro to head out onto the spectacular green-blue seas. The coastline here is stunningly beautiful, but the seas can be tragically misleading: beautiful and still, or thunderous and deadly when the winds whip up in the channel and the steely blue waters turn to white. As the boat chugged out past the breakwaters into open sea, I felt the surge of the swell lifting and dropping the boat in a gentle rhythm, a feeling that sailors in these parts have experienced for many hundreds of years. Turning right, the boat chugged manfully along a westerly course, following the rugged and barren coastline while I marvelled at the spectacular cliffs that border this part of the Cornish coast.

Riddled with caves created from eons of erosion from winds and waters, I wondered if it were possible that the great sea monster Morgawr lived in one of these dark, wet overhangs, or possibly in an undiscovered undersea cave. And, given the water traffic in this area over the centuries, I found it unsurprising that people have reported strange creatures in the sea. Surely, if one were to come across such a beast, it would be in these cold, ancient waters?

The boat continued to chug happily along the Cornish coastline. Above me, the sun was shining warmly in the early spring, and the water was now a peculiar ice-like blue. An immense seagull circled around the boat like the albatross in Coleridge's *Ancient Mariner,* and I found myself thinking that this truly was a land of wonder: a land of piskies, mermaids, sea monsters, ghosts, Arthurian legends, and the more believable pirates, smugglers and ancient ruins.

But today the pirates and smugglers are long gone, replaced by tens of thousands of tourists who flock to these shores every summer. Do these visitors see and experience the supernatural and paranormal? Do their video recorders and digital cameras pick up strange anomalies in the seas, the lonely ramparts of ruined castles, or on the wilds of the moors? Whatever the case, I saw no sea monsters, and my only companion—apart from my partner and a particularly crusty Cornish fisherman—was a rather angry-looking gull, as I had no fish to feed to it.

Still, although my quest went unfulfilled, in February 2015 a number of people sighted what appeared to be a twenty-foot-long reptile swimming in waters off the coast of Devon and Cornwall. Indeed, one of the witnesses managed to photograph the creature which, to be honest, could be construed as a whale.

Allan Jones, a university technician, who took the staggering photos, said: "At one point it was near a boat and it looked about the same length—about twenty feet long." And he added, "I've never seen anything like it— the first thing that struck me was that it looked just like a huge crocodile."

Maybe, just maybe, Morgawr had made her presence felt once again?

But it's not just remote and desolate Scottish isles or ancient channels where sea monsters seemingly reside, as one of the most terrifying encounters of mysterious sea creatures was by schoolteacher Alphonsus Mullaney and his young son, also called Alphonsus, who were fishing one day in March 1962 at Lough Dubh in County Galway, Ireland. Mullaney later told a local newspaper, "Suddenly there was a tugging on the line. I thought it might be caught on a root, so I took it gently. It did not give. I hauled it slowly ashore, and the line snapped. I was examining the line when the lad screamed. Then I saw the animal. It was not a seal or anything I had ever seen. It had, for instance, short, thick legs and a hippo face. It was as big as a cow or an ass, square-faced, with small ears and a white pointed horn on its snout. It was dark grey in colour, and covered with bristles or short hair, like a pig."

After the two terrified fishers fled, a party of locals returned to the spot with guns, but no trace of the monster was to be found. However, after the event, both father and son Mullaney shunned all media interviews, with the father attempting to distance himself and his son from the experience. As such, it would appear that the sighting was genuine, whatever it may have been. As for the creature itself, no further sightings have been reported and, as it bears no resemblance to any other lake monster reported or witnessed, it remains a complete enigma, which leads us nicely onto our next chapter.

Chapter Two

Creatures of Lochs, Lakes and River

Whereas so-called sea monsters could conceivably exist due to the sheer immenseness of the earth's oceans, the same could not be said of strange creatures in freshwater bodies. And yet, like the great lakes of northern America and Scandinavia, the British Isles have a wealth of lake monster sightings, from the very familiar at Loch Ness to reports of a strange beast recently filmed in the Thames.

And apart from these, there are many more reports of secretive and enigmatic creatures within the lakes, rivers and lochs of Britain, dating as far back as recorded history and probably further. Some of these reports are indelibly entwined with old folklore stories about dragons and mermaids, while others, more modern sightings, are often attributed to unidentified real creatures, including extinct dinosaurs. Having said this, there is little doubt that, like sea monsters, strange creatures are regularly seen in numerous bodies of water. What they are, however, is much more difficult to ascertain. Indeed, some believe them not to be flesh-and-blood creatures as such, but more supernatural. Whatever the case, they keep appearing and will probably continue to do so, in various guises, in the future.

However, before we look at the phenomenon of lake and river monsters, I have to put forward a disclaimer: I have witnessed what I thought at the time was an unidentified creature in Loch Ness.

Many years ago, in the 1970s, whilst travelling through northern England and Scotland on holiday with my parents and brothers, we stopped at Inverness, a smallish town situated at the mouth of the River Ness, which flows from nearby Loch Ness, at the southwestern extremity of the Moray Firth. The city itself lies at the end of the Great Glen, with Loch Ness, Loch Ashie and Loch Duntelchaig to the west. In hindsight, I really can't remember much about the place—and yet, standing there on the edge of the river, I saw something large and dark swimming against the current.

Watching intently, I noticed that it had a smooth, rounded head about the size of a large dog and a slightly rounded, fattish body. Indeed, at one stage it appeared to roll over in the water, revealing a brief flash of what I thought were flippers. Fascinated, I called my family over, and together we could hardly believe what we were seeing. Could this really be the legendary Loch Ness Monster? After all, this *was* the River Ness, which is connected to Loch Ness. Surely not? But there, in the water, was a creature: blackish, with fins and a rounded head.

And then, quite suddenly, it stopped swimming and sat up in the water, revealing its head and most of its body, and showing quite plainly that it was no prehistoric leftover from Triassic times. In fact, it was simply a seal.

Looking back at the incident, I can truly say that, at the time, I believed I could have been watching the Loch Ness Monster. The creature in the water was unidentified, it had some of the characteristics of the monster, and I was next to the River Ness. Everything pointed to it being only one thing: the Loch Ness Monster. And if the creature had not revealed itself to be a seal, then I would have spent the rest of my life believing that I had truly seen the Loch Ness Monster, which clearly shows how suggestion and misinterpretation can play a big part in the sighting of strange creatures and beings, not only for river monsters, but equally in the case of ghosts, Black Dogs, fairies, goblins, UFOs, Bunyips, Yowies, Bigfoot and the like.

But this is not to say that these things do not exist: reports are so numerous, and often so similar, that not all could be mistaken identity, suggestion or pure fantasy. A colleague of mine, Tim the Yowieman, a respected writer and internationally renowned cryptonaturalist, has also had a strange encounter on this loch.

In the late 1990s Tim found himself in Scotland researching material for his book *The Adventures of Tim the Yowie Man* and, as the Loch Ness Monster is probably the world's greatest mystery animal, he decided to try his luck at photographing the elusive beast.

After hiring a boat, Tim set out onto the dark waters of Loch Ness with, as he puts it, "the stale-tasting waters of the loch being scooped off the surface by scuds of driving sleet and then slammed into my bare face, which was blue from the cold".

Apparently, a thick mist descended upon the loch but then, as quickly as it arrived, the mist, wind and sleet disappeared revealing, some ten–fifteen metres away on the port side of the boat, "what appeared to be the neck of a large serpent-like creature".

After recovering from the initial shock, Tim grabbed for his camera but, after taking one shot, "all of a sudden there was nothing in the water except for a few ripples. It had vanished."

Later, upon reviewing the photograph, Tim found that whatever it was he saw had been obscured by a slight mist. The photograph was, essentially, useless. On reflection, he has suggested that the creature may have simply been a deer that had wandered into the loch and then become disoriented in the mist. But, then again, he also suggests that it just *may* have been the legendary Nessie.

Given that Tim is somewhat sceptical as to the existence of a large prehistoric beast swimming around in the dark waters of the loch, what are we to make of the masses of other sightings that have occurred? Are these all simply deluded people who have had one too many whiskys in local pubs? Or, have they simply mistaken what they have seen—for instance, a stag swimming, or a log floating by in the fog?

The legend of Loch Ness begins in the very mists of time. Written in the seventh century, the *Life of St Columba* describes how St Columba was staying in the land of the Picts when he came across some locals burying a man by the River Ness. They explained that he had been swimming across the river when a beast had attacked him and dragged him under. Although they could not save the unfortunate man, they at least managed to retrieve his body. Hearing this, St Columba sent one of his followers to swim the river. The beast duly rose from the depths and headed for the stricken man. Making the Sign of the Cross, St Columba commanded, "Go no further. Do not touch the man. Go back at once." The beast immediately halted and fled in terror leaving Columba's men and the pagan Picts praising God for the miracle.

Believers in the Loch Ness Monster story will often point out that this ancient chronicle is proof of the legend being verified over time, even if the account took place on the River Ness and not on the actual loch itself. However, it has been suggested that the tale is simply a story to illustrate to unbelievers how great the Christian god was in comparison to pagan gods of the time. Having said this, there could, still, be a shed of truth in all of it, given that a walrus could probably swim up the river from the sea and, if angry enough or provoked, would almost certainly attack a man.

But if there are problems with the verification of St Columba's story due to the ravages of time, there is certainly no such problem with other sightings, including in 1933, when two sensational stories hit the press.

On 22 July 1933, George Spicer and his wife got the shock of their lives when "a most extraordinary form of animal" shuffled across the road in front of their car. They described the creature as having a large body—about four feet high and twenty-five feet long—and a long, narrow neck (slightly thicker than an elephant's trunk), and as long as the ten to twelve-foot width of the road. The neck was also reported to have a number of undulations in it. Surprisingly, they saw no limbs, possibly because of a dip in the road obscuring the animal's lower portion, but it lurched across the road towards the loch—about twenty yards away—leaving a trail of broken undergrowth in its wake. And this in itself is compelling, as the broken and crushed undergrowth proved that the couple had witnessed *something*, something large enough to crush the vegetation that lined the banks of the loch.

Then, in August of the same year, a motorcyclist by the name of Arthur Grant claimed to have almost hit a strange creature whilst riding on the northeastern shore late one night. Grant claimed that he saw a small head attached to a long neck and that the creature crossed in front of him and then into the loch. Grant stated that he dismounted and followed the creature but could only see ripples on the water's surface.

Then, in 1934, a stunning photograph, purporting to show the monster, emerged. Known as the 'Surgeon's Photograph', it clearly shows a long-necked creature wallowing in the loch. The photographer, Robert Wilson, a London-based gynaecologist, claimed he was looking at the loch when he saw the monster and consequently grabbed his camera and snapped five photos. After the film was developed, only two exposures were useable, the first clearly showing the creature and the second blurry and indistinct.

The sensational photo was published in the *Daily Mail*

in April 1934, although—curiously—Wilson refused to have his name associated with it. At the time, some questioned its authenticity due to the unusually small ripples in the water, which did not seem quite right for such a large creature. Further analysis of the uncropped photo fostered more doubt, but the photo was generally thought to show a large unknown plesiosaur-like creature frolicking on the loch's surface.

In 1979 it was claimed that the photograph was that of an elephant—although what an elephant was doing swimming in Loch Ness was never adequately explained (it *is* suspected that a circus bathed elephants in the Loch in the early 1900s). Indeed, palaeontologist and painter Neil Clark noted, "The reason why we see elephants in Loch Ness is that circuses used to go along the road to Inverness and have a little rest at the side of the loch and allow the animals to go and have a little swim around." Others argued that it was a diving bird of some description or even an otter. Whatever the case, it became the most famous and well- known of all Loch Ness Monster photos.

That is, until 1994, when the image was revealed as a hoax. In reality, it was a miniature model monster mounted on a toy submarine and built by Christian Spurling, the son-in-law of Marmaduke Wetherell, a big-game hunter who had previously been ridiculed by the *Daily Mail* and harboured a grudge. With the help of his son Ian, Maurice Chambers, an insurance agent, as well as Wilson, they managed to create one of the biggest hoaxes of the twentieth century.

Oddly, reputed Loch Ness Monster researcher Tim

Dinsdale disputed that the photo was a hoax and claimed that, "Upon really close examination, there are certain rather obscure features in the picture which have a profound significance."

Dinsdale noted that there was a solid object breaking the surface to the right of the neck, and to the left and behind the neck there was another mark of some sort, and that, although it was impossible to discern what the objects were, they were probably a part of the creature.

Another feature that Dinsdale noted was the smaller ripples behind the neck, which seemed to have been caused after the neck broke the surface. Dinsdale emphatically stated that this was a part of the animal underwater, behind the neck, and therefore proof that the photo was, in fact, genuine.

In another twist, Alastair Boyd, one of the researchers who uncovered the hoax, argued the Loch Ness Monster was probably real, and that although the 'Surgeon's Photograph' was a definite hoax, this did not mean that all the photos, eyewitness reports, and video or film footage of the monster were also hoaxes. He also argued, with good reason, that a hoaxed photo was not a reason to dismiss eyewitness reports and other evidence.

But this is not where the story of the Loch Ness Monster ends. If anything, the 'Surgeon's Photograph', as famous as it is, is only a small part of the rich tapestry of stories, eyewitness accounts, videos and film footage that exists to suggest that maybe, just maybe, the Loch Ness Monster, whatever it is, could be real.

In 1938 GE Taylor, a South African on holiday, managed to take three minutes' footage of something on the loch. Sadly, only a single frame of this film was ever released and, although it was later declared as positive evidence of a large creature living in the loch, its non-release to the public will always create doubt and scepticism about the footage.

Then, in 1960, Tim Dinsdale filmed what appeared to be a hump crossing the water and leaving a strong and extremely visible wake. Whereas some declared the object to be animate, others pointed out that it simply looked like a boat filmed from a great distance. Indeed, it was claimed that when the contrast was increased a person could be seen piloting the boat, although this has never been conclusively proven.

And so, like the Taylor film, Dinsdale's footage was seen as inconclusive until 1993, when a documentary digitally enhanced the Dinsdale film, and a shadow was noticed in the negative that was not evident in the positive. By enhancing and overlaying frames, it was found that something that appeared to be the body, the rear flippers, and one or two additional humps of a plesiosaur-like body were evident in the footage.

Aside from numerous sightings, there have been exerted efforts to prove the existence of the monster. Starting in 1934, the Sir Edward Mountain expedition (which consisted of nothing more than a group of men with binoculars watching the loch), and continuing into the 1960s, when an explosion of scientifically based expeditions was conducted.

From the aptly named Loch Ness Phenomena Bureau of 1962–1972 to the Andrew Carroll sonar study of 1968, and even submersible expeditions with small, remotely controlled manned submarines, the loch came under intense scrutiny. By the 1970s, researchers employed hydrophones to listen to what was happening beneath the murky waters. Although all expeditions had some success, the evidence still remained sketchy until a group of researchers, led by an American by the name of Robert Rines, managed to come up with some stunning and quite compelling underwater photographs of what appeared to be a large plesiosaur-like creature in the peat-filled waters of the loch.

At first, Rines and his team managed to take two rather vague but intriguing images of what appeared to be a rhomboid flipper in different positions, thus indicating movement. Sceptics were quick to point out that the blurry underwater photos could easily be air bubbles released by the camera or the fin of a large fish. However, on the basis of these photos, British naturalist Sir Peter Scott—who was knighted in 1973 for his contribution to the conservation of wild animals—announced, in 1975, that the scientific name for the monster was now *Nessiteras rhombopteryx*, Greek for 'The Ness Monster with diamond-shaped fin'.

Humorously, Scottish politician Nicholas Fairbairn later pointed out that the new scientific name was also an anagram for 'Monster hoax by Sir Peter S.'.

Whatever the case, the work done by Rines and his team was painstaking and thorough, examining the loch with sonar for unusual underwater activity and using a submersible camera attached to a high-powered light source, designed to penetrate the murky depths of the loch. If anything was detected on sonar, the lights and cameras would be turned on in an attempt to capture an image of whatever had tripped it.

Remarkably, more photos were obtained, including some that resembled a plesiosaur and another that appeared to show a head. Some more photos of flippers were also taken, and in one shot two plesiosaur-like creatures can be seen at the periphery of the light.

In addition to the photographs, the Rines expedition also picked up numerous large sonar hits, up to six to nine metres in length and moving. Examination of the data proposed that the shape was a highly flexible laterally flattened tail or the misinterpreted return from two animals swimming together. As late as 2001, Robert Rines's Academy of Applied Science videoed a powerful V-shaped wake traversing the still water on a calm day, adding more speculation as to the existence of a large unknown creature in the loch.

Apart from Rines and his numerous expeditions, other scientific expeditions have turned up intriguing, if not compelling, evidence for the creature. In 1987, Operation Deep Scan deployed twenty-four boats, all equipped with echo sounder equipment, to scan the waters of the loch. It was reported that after one sweep the scientists had made sonar contact with a large unidentified object of unusual size and strength. To be sure, the researchers returned to the same point and rescanned the area, with the results seemingly pointing to debris at the bottom of the loch, although three of these pictures were of moving debris. It has been suggested that these echo sounder hits could have been seals, as they appeared to be about the same size of the objects detected.

A particular result, however, was recorded near Urquhart Bay at a depth of six hundred feet, when the sonar return showed a large moving object. One of the researchers commented, "There's something here that we don't understand, and there's something here that's larger than a fish, maybe some species that hasn't been detected before. I don't know."

In 2003, even the BBC were in on the act, sponsoring a full search of the loch using sonar and satellite tracking. Sadly, all they found was a small buoy and, despite high hopes, the scientists involved could only conclude that the whole Loch Ness story was just a myth.

But even with the tantalising, if less than encouraging, evidence supplied by sonar, underwater cameras and the like, reports of the creature have continued to pile up over the years.

For instance, on 9 April 1996, Bill Kinder from Lancashire observed a black shiny object rise out of the water just north of Fort Augustus and move along the loch surface, leaving a ten-metre wake. On the same day, the Ling family from London reported seeing two humps rise out of the water and leave a long trail. Just a day later, two large brown shapes, ten feet in diameter and three feet apart, were spotted by a couple 200 metres offshore from Urquhart Castle, before the shapes travelled across the loch and disappeared.

Even as late as 2007, Sidney Wilson, on holiday from Nottingham, took a cruise on the loch when, approaching Urquhart Castle, he saw what appeared to be a large wake left by two power boats. Wilson took a photo of the wake and, upon inspection, realised that the second photo appeared to show a head and fin.

Again in 2007, a remarkable two-minute video clip shows what could be construed as a long, black creature swimming just below the water surface. At one stage, its head breaks the water as it propels itself along. Filmed by Gordon Holmes from Yorkshire, he said: "About two hundred yards away from me, I could see something in the water. It was definitely a creature propelling itself through the water. It was fairly bubbling along the water. It was streaking along."

With sightings of the legendary beast seeming almost common place, what are we to think? Is it possible that all the sightings are simply cases of mistaken identity? For instance, a large eel, otters, seals, a swimming deer, an upturned boat or a seriously lost walrus? Perhaps the sightings are nothing more than that of a tree or a boat wake, or, because of a trick of light, an optical illusion? Maybe the sightings are all these and more, given that these days the Loch Ness region seems to thrive almost exclusively on the monster trade. Whatever the case, sightings in recent years seem to have subsided—and yet, one must ask, can all of those people over so many years be wrong?

Interestingly, Robert Rines theorised in 2008 that the monster may be dead, a victim of global warming—even though there is little evidence to suggest that the loch itself has been affected in any way by climate change. Rhine's last expedition, using sonar and underwater cameras, found no evidence of the creature whatsoever, either living or dead.

In 2015, I travelled to Scotland with the express purpose of staying at Loch Ness so I could explore the surroundings and the legend from a first-person perspective. Not only did this include a cruise on the loch, complete with sonar readings, but also a trip to Urquhart Castle and a visit to the Loch Ness Centre. Apart from that, my hotel room, in an old Victorian hunting lodge just outside Fort Augustus, looked out towards Cherry Island, actually an ancient Iron Age crannog sitting on the edge of the loch.

The loch itself lies along the Great Glen Fault, which forms a line of weakness in the rocks that have been excavated by glacial erosion, forming the Great Glen and the basins of Loch Lochy, Loch Oich and Loch Ness. It is approximately thirty-seven kilometres long and sits sixteen metres above sea level. It is connected at the southern end by the River Oich and part of the Caledonian Canal to Loch Oich. At its northern end, the Bona Narrows opens out into Loch Dochfour, which feeds the River Ness and a further section of canal to Inverness. Water visibility is extremely low due to a high peat content in the surrounding soil.

It is the second-largest loch by surface area, but due to

its incredible depth, it is the largest by volume in the British Isles. Its deepest point is 230 metres, making it the second-deepest loch in Scotland after Loch Morar and, in all, it contains more fresh water than all the lakes in England and Wales combined. Considering all this, there is little wonder why it seems to be a magical place and one where such a monster could exist. Sadly, on this occasion, Nessie remained hidden from my sight, although I did manage to take a number of interesting photographs of boat wakes, which looked surprisingly like 'humps'.

Amusingly, in April 2016, Adrian Shine announced to BBC News Scotland that, "We have found a monster, but not the one many people might have expected." The ten-metre-long model, from the 1970 film *The Private Life of Sherlock Holmes*, was discovered 180 metres down on the loch's bed by an underwater robot. Shine added that, "The model was built with a neck and two humps and taken alongside a pier for filming of portions of the film in 1969. The director did not want the humps and asked that they be removed, despite warnings, I suspect from the rest of the production, that this would affect its buoyancy. And the inevitable happened. The model sank."

The Private Life of Sherlock Holmes was directed by Billy Wilder and starred Christopher Lee as Holmes's brother, Mycroft, and Robert Stephens as Holmes. In the film, a woman persuades Holmes to look for her missing husband, and the search takes him to Loch Ness and an encounter with the monster. However, it turns out—in the film—that the 'monster' is actually a submarine.

But Nessie, as she or he is affectionately known, is not the only well-known lake monster that haunts large inland waterways. Also in Scotland, a fearsome beast known as Morag is reputed to live in the cold depths of Loch Morar. Sightings of Morag date back to 1887 and include multiple witnesses. Like the Loch Ness Monster, several expeditions have been launched to establish the existence of the creature but, thus far, no evidence for an unknown, large aquatic creature has been found. Having said this, early accounts of the monster are not uncommon.

Loch Morar is located just seventy miles from Loch Ness and was created by glacial movement during the last ice age. It is British Isles' deepest loch, with a maximum depth of over three hundred metres and, unlike most Scottish lochs—which are stained a murky brown colour from peat deposits—the waters of Loch Morar are crystal clear, due in part to the sheer rock cliffs that surround the loch.

Sightings of this creature, dubbed Morag by the locals, go as far back as the mid-1800s, when residents and visitors to the region began to report sightings of undulating humps. And, not surprisingly for superstitious folk, sightings of the humps were considered to be an ominous warning of death.

Alexander Carmichael, folklorist, antiquarian and author, gathered a vast amount of folklore, local traditions, natural history observations, antiquarian data, and material objects from people throughout the Scottish Highlands at the turn of the last century, including stories of Morag, the scripts of which were discovered recently at the University of Edinburgh library. However, rather than shedding light on the subject, Carmichael's writings, if anything, muddy the waters by painting a conflicting view of the monster. On the one hand, Morag is portrayed as a mermaid-like character with flowing hair, while another account describes her as a grim reaper-type character, whose sighting was widely viewed as an omen of death.

In the one script, Carmichael states that, "Morag is always seen before a death and before a drowning." However, a second text reads: "There is a creature in Loch Morar and she is called Morag. She is never seen, save when one of the hereditary people of the place dies."

Having said this, Carmichael also notes that, "Morag is peculiar to Loch Morar. She is seen in broad daylight and by many persons, including church persons. She appears in a black heap or ball, slowing and deliberately rising in the water and moving along like a boat waterlogged."

However, a final description, written by Carmichael at a later date, sees Morag retain the connection with death but also take on more human characteristics, more akin to a mermaid than a prehistoric monster: "Like the other water deities, she is half-human, half-fish. The lower portion of her body is in the form of a grilse and the upper in the form of a small woman of highly developed breasts, with long, flowing yellow hair falling down her snow-white back and breast. She is represented as being fair, beautiful and very timid, and never seen, save when one of the Morar family dies or when the clan falls in battle."

As we can plainly see, Morag, now considered a lake monster similar to the Loch Ness Monster and many other lake monsters reported around the world, once took on an otherworldly aspect—very much more akin to mermaids or sprites or other freshwater-dwelling deities.

Although Carmichael never claimed to actually see the monster and, in all probability, only spent a short time at the loch itself, he seems to have used a local by the name of Ewan MacDougall as his main source of information. However, his texts, discovered by a Dr Donald Stewart in 2011, appear to show that he truly believed in the monster, whatever form it had taken. As Stewart commented, "Clearly, there's something going on in Loch Morar, whatever it is," and, "People make sense of it in different ways, depending on who sees it, what they're feeling at the time and how the story comes down from tradition afterwards."

As we have noted, the first recorded sighting of Morag was in 1887, while in 1948 nine people in a boat claimed to have seen a twenty-foot-long creature in the loch.

In 1974, two men claimed to have accidentally hit the creature in their boat; it was said to have disappeared after one of them hit it with an oar, while his companion opened fire with a rifle. Whether or not the creature was hit is unknown. However, in 1970 and 1971, the Loch Ness Investigation Bureau considered the Morag legend strong enough to conduct research on the loch during what they called the Loch Morar Survey, and on 14 July 1970, team member and marine biologist Neil Bass claimed to have spotted a hump-shaped black object moving in the water.

In the same year, two members involved in the expedition, Elizabeth Montgomery Campbell and David Solomon, published a well-regarded book entitled *The Search for Morag,* which recalled the tale of John MacVarish, the barman at the Morar Hotel, who claimed he saw Morag on 27 August 1968, while fishing on the loch: "I never saw any features, no eyes or anything like that. It was a snake-like head, very small compared to the size of the neck—flattish, a flat type of head. It was very dark, nearly black. It looked as if it was paddling itself along."

On April 3 1971, Ewen Gillies, a lifelong resident of the loch and whose house over looked the water, claimed to have seen Morag after being alerted by his twelve-year-old son John, who noticed a disturbance in the loch while walking along a road near the shore. It was a clear, sunny morning around 11.00 a.m. and, as Gillies looked out, he saw a huge creature in the water, not quite half a mile away. He later described it as having a head barely distinguishable from its three-to-four-foot-long neck with two or three humps along its back, moving slowly in the water. The skin was black and its estimated length was about thirty feet.

Also in the 1970s, Adrian Shine, renowned Scottish naturalist and Loch Ness Project leader, led an expedition to Loch Morar in hope of gathering evidence to support the existence of Morag. Using a submersible that he produced himself, Shine hoped to take advantage of Loch Morar's clear water to observe any large creatures in the loch. However, his efforts bore little or no conclusive evidence.

While there is no doubt that Loch Morar, unlike Loch Ness, possesses an adequate food supply to support a population of large animals, it is unclear exactly *what* the creature might be. The majority of sightings describe a creature with a remarkable resemblance to a long-extinct plesiosaur, much like the Loch Ness Monster, which of course leads us to a conclusion that the excitement generated at Loch Ness over the years has somehow led to people misinterpreting what they are *actually* seeing in Loch Morar. And yet, surely, we could use the same similarity to point out that, if one of these creatures existed in Loch Ness, then surely another could exist in Loch Morar?

And if such animals were to have survived from prehistoric times, they would have had to adapt to far colder water temperatures than their ancestors are thought to have lived in. As a result, biologist Roy P. Mackal has suggested that Morag, the Loch Ness Monster, and the other so-called monsters are, in fact, zeuglodons: a primitive whale believed to have been extinct for over twenty million years. Other theories that have regularly seen the light of day include walruses, sharks, seals, eels, deer, and even floating logs—and yet, if one is to recall the descriptions of both the Loch Ness and Loch Morar monsters, one would note that they obviously have nothing in common with modern creatures.

But if Morag and Nessie have both been misidentified, then what of our next strange and extremely contemporary report? That of a creature in the River Thames itself.

In April 2016, mysterious footage emerged on YouTube showing what appeared to be a large animate object making its way through the greyish waters of the Thames near the O2 Arena. Incredibly, it can be seen surfacing briefly before sinking back down and disappearing. The video footage was taken by Penn Plate as he travelled on the Emirates Air Line, a cable car trip near Greenwich. He stated: "This was on the cable car in Greenwich yesterday. Something huge was moving under the water and then briefly surfaced. Are there whales in the Thames? Or is it some weird submarine?"

Remarkably, only a few days after the first sighting, *The Telegraph*, among other media outlets, ran another story including an eighteen-second video of what appeared to be the same humped creature, again swimming against the current. And to make things even more interesting, a day later footage of another apparent sighting of the creature occurred near the Thames' flood barriers, this time a dark shape that briefly surfaced before sliding back into the murky waters with a slight splash.

Of course, this sighting wouldn't be the first time an unusual creature has been spotted in the capital's river as, in January 2006, a northern bottle-nosed whale spent several days in the Thames after becoming lost. Sadly, the whale died of dehydration while trying to make its way back out to sea. And, as noted by the Zoological Society of London, more than 2000 seals and 450 porpoises and dolphins have been spotted in the Thames in the past decade.

But it's not just distant Scottish lochs and the Thames where we can find so-called monsters: legend suggests that Lake Windermere in Cumbria in the Lake District may also hold some secrets.

Windermere is the largest natural lake in England. It is classed as a ribbon lake and was formed in a glacial trough after the retreat of ice at the start of the current interglacial period. It is one of the country's most popular places for holidays and summer homes and has been since the arrival of the railways in the 1840s. It is also believed to hold a lake monster, similar to that in Loch Ness and affectionately known as 'Bownessie'.

Sightings of 'Bownessie' are few, especially in comparison to its more famous Scottish counterpart. However, a number of eyewitness reports and photos have emerged, and while some are most probably faked, others remain quite inexplicable, especially one taken by an IT expert, Tom Pickles, on 11 February of 2011.

The photograph, which clearly shows an object with three humps breaching the surface of the lake, was taken on camera phone while Pickles was kayaking on the lake as part of a team-building exercise with his IT company, and it is said to be the best evidence yet of what some claim is a monster lurking beneath the dark waters of the lake.

Pickles, who was with a companion, Sarah Harrington, said he saw an animal the size of three cars speed past him on the lake and then managed to watch it for about twenty seconds. He commented that it was "petrifying and we paddled back to the shore straight away. At first, I thought it was a dog and then saw it was much bigger and moving really quickly, at about ten miles per hour."

He added: "Each hump was moving in a rippling motion and it was swimming fast. I could tell it was much bigger underneath from the huge shadow around it."

A photo expert from Lancaster, David Farnell, said of the remarkable image: "It does look like a real photo but, because it's been taken on a phone, the file size is too small to really tell whether it has been altered on Photoshop or not."

As such, sceptics remain unconvinced that something so large could exist in the eleven-mile-long lake, and Dr Ian Winfield, an ecologist from the University of Lancaster, stated: "It's possible that it's a catfish from Eastern Europe and people are misjudging the size, but there is no known fish as large as the descriptions we're hearing that could be living in Windermere."

However, he also added: "We run echo sounding surveys every month and have never found anything."

And so, we are left with a question: does a monster of large proportions exist in the lake? And while most would be sceptical, and have reason to be so, others are not so sure.

In July of 2006, Steve and Elaine Burnip from Hebden

Bridge in Yorkshire, were standing at Watbarrow Point when they described seeing three humps breaking the water and travelling in a straight line. One hump was described as a head, and Steve Burnip commented that "it wasn't a wave or boat wake … It looked like a giant eel and was twenty-feet long." He also stated that it was faster than a rowing boat, but not as fast as a motorboat.

Sadly, Burnip seemed very reluctant to give the photograph to the press, which immediately raised suspicions as to its real origin. However, Jon Downes of the Centre for Fortean Zoology, an organisation dedicated to cryptozoology, managed to view the image, and commented: "He showed us the original of the photograph he had taken, still on his digital camera, and zoomed in. What had been merely discoloration in the water on the version that had been rather badly reproduced by the *Westmorland Gazette*, were actually what appeared to be quite sizeable humps. We hope that, as time goes by, we shall be able to persuade Steve to let us have a copy for our own use."

Also in July 2006, a Mr and Mrs Gaskell, who were cruising near Ambleside at the north end of the lake, saw what they described as a large animal jumping in the wake of their vessel "which looked like a seal or dolphin without the fin, leaving a large wake and ripples".

Then, in February 2007, photographer Linden Adams was walking in the area with his wife when he spotted something in the water. He said it appeared to be fifty feet long when compared to boats nearby, and he managed to get a remarkably clear photograph of the anomaly, which was subsequently published in a number of newspapers.

Adams commented: "The water was unbelievably peaceful and then this huge thing appeared, diving and thrashing around," and that "it dwarfed everything. It was jaw-dropping."

Adams apparently took a pair of binoculars from his wife to get a better view and commented that he could see "this huge dark thing moving in the water. I didn't know what it was but it had a head like a labrador dog, only much, much bigger. I know the lake well and this was no freak wave."

Tellingly, he added: "I was a sceptic before but this has really opened my mind to what might be in the lake."

Dr Charles Paxton, a marine biologist at the University of St Andrews and an expert in the discovery of new sea creatures, later studied the photographs and concluded, "What the photograph shows is very intriguing, and I wouldn't rule out any possibilities. New species of water creatures are still being discovered. I will be going to Lake Windermere very soon and will be spending some time trying to find any new creatures." However, he added the caveat, "But until someone brings this creature onto dry land in a net, we won't have proof."

Later, in July 2007, the crew of a boat which was moored at the north end of the lake described how something huge slammed into the six-tonne yacht, causing it to rock and wake the crew. The local press picked up on this and dubbed it a '*Jaws*-style' attack.

Bownessie then appeared to calm down for a while until, in July 2009, Thomas Noblett, managing director of the Langdale Chase Hotel, was swimming close to Wray Castle at 7.00 a.m. when he was swamped by a huge swell that appeared from nowhere. He and swimming trainer Andrew Tighe, who was paddling in a boat beside him, were the only people on the lake.

Noblett, who had been training on the lake for four hours every day in preparation for a Channel swim, said that the incident had made him reconsider the legend of the Windermere Monster: "We had gotten up early and Windermere was crystal clear. The lake was totally empty apart from us, and all I could hear was the slapping of my arm against the water. All of a sudden, this wave just hit us. Andrew said, 'Where the hell did that come from?' and it made the boat rock from side to side."

Treading water in the middle of the lake, Noblett watched as two large waves sped towards either shore: "It was like a big bow wave; a three-foot swell, at least. There were two, as if a speedboat had sped past, but there were no boats on the lake."

Not surprisingly, Noblett now approaches his swimming in a much different light after the incident: "I always look forward to swimming in Windermere; now I'm starting to get the fear. Twice I have looked down and seen fish, but only small trout. The reeds sometimes scare you, because they suddenly appear like triffids."

Interestingly, this event was recalled by Noblett on the television programme, *The Lakes (Series 2),* hosted by Rory McGrath.

Later, in February 2011, Brian and June Arton from Hovingham in North Yorkshire were at the Beech Hill Hotel off Newby Bridge Road when, as Brian Arton put it: "We'd just checked into our hotel room at around 4.00 p.m. when I opened the veranda doors and saw something about three hundred yards away in the middle of the lake. I joked to my wife: 'There's the Loch Ness Monster', as it had humps, but I thought it had to be a pontoon or a very strange-shaped buoy."

This was later reported in the *Westmorland Gazette,* where it was reported: "If it was a log or a buoy it wouldn't have disappeared like that out of sight," and, "I know people are cynical, but what I saw was very clear undulating shapes against the background of the water."

The Centre for Fortean Zoology carried out a number of expeditions to the lake between 2006 and 2010 but sadly came up with little evidence to suggest that the creature existed. Jonathon Downes commented: "Our theory is that they are giant eels, which occur once or twice in a generation but are nowhere near as big as people say. When eels reach sexual maturity, they swim down to the sea, migrate to the Sargasso Sea, mate, spawn and die. We believe that, occasionally, an eel is born sterile, so it doesn't have the biological imperative to migrate; it stays in freshwater and carries on eating and gets enormous. European eels are not supposed to get bigger than four feet but there is, or was, a five-foot-plus one in Blackpool Tower Aquarium of all places. I think that once or twice in a generation in a large body of water like Windermere or Loch Ness, a specimen of eight–twelve feet could be living. We have found eyewitnesses, but the rest is exaggeration or potentially fraud. If there is anything there, it has to be a fish, and basically that means eel, pike, or possibly sturgeon. In my long and chequered career, I have found that there is usually a sensible explanation for everything—not always, but very much usually."

Having said that, an expedition by Dean Maynard to the lake in September 2010 turned up some interesting film footage. John McKeown of Lakes TV, who was filming shots of the lake for a documentary about Maynard's investigation of the creature, picked up something he claimed to be twenty metres in length, breaking the water in a V shape. Interestingly, the novel *Giant Killer Eels* by Stuart Neild, published in 2010, is set in the Lake District and features Bownessie-like monsters in Windermere and Lake Unsworth.

But if Bownessie had been somewhat written off, in September 2014 the public were again alerted to the possibility that a monster of sorts may exist in the lake: Ellie Williams, a twenty-four-year-old photographer, picked up a strange image that appeared to show a stereotypical Loch Ness Monster-style beast in the lake. The photograph was taken by a hi-tech camera called an Autographer, which takes photos automatically throughout the day without human help. Speaking about the incident, Williams said, "When I set up the Autographer at Lake Windermere, it was just business as usual to take some lovely photos of the lake and wildlife. So, I put it on a tripod to automatically capture some nice shots. When I reviewed all the images later, at first, I thought it might have been a swan or a goose, as I was looking at the image quite small on my smartphone."

According to Williams, the image has not been manipulated and is genuine, as the pictures taken two minutes before and after are completely monster-free. However, James Ebdon, of the Autographer camera company, said: "On closer look, we thought it could be a larger animal like a horse with a saddle pack or something. Then we wondered if it was an old giant eel or catfish, as seen on TV documentaries. Initially we were excited, then sceptical, and then we started laughing. Who knows what it is—maybe some kids messing about? Whatever it is, we will leave it to the experts."

But if there is doubt about the existence of a monster in the depths of Lake Windermere, then there are absolutely no doubts about the existence of our next creature, whose carcass was found by a number of walkers in August 2015 on the banks of Hollingworth Lake in Rochdale, Greater Manchester.

Dubbed the 'Roch Ness Monster', the strange five-foot fish had a mouth full of razor-sharp teeth and sparked an intense online debate over what loiters in Britain's lakes, with one person suggesting that he could fit his entire fist inside the animal's mouth.

Jonny Beckett, a sales worker, said: "I was just on a romantic walk with my partner, Suzanne, and I was stunned when I saw it. I thought it was a crocodile or some ancient creature, and I immediately took a photo of it. It looked huge, about five feet in length."

Many online users suggested the beast was nothing more than an ordinary pike, given that they are regularly found in the 130-acre reservoir and have been known to grow up to four feet. However, the creature has been enough to put off regular visitors, with local resident Carole Ann Gleeson stating, "It's bloody horrible. I won't paddle in the lake again, that's for sure."

But if the so-called 'Roch Ness Monster' was nothing but an immense pike, then what of our next two creatures, which span the gap between mythology and reality and can also be traced through references in British and Celtic folklore.

The horse eel is just one of the many weird creatures that are said to inhabit the water ways of Ireland. They have been sighted all over the Connemara bogs and other places across Ireland and are known for keeping turf-cutters and children away from the safer shallows and land at sunset. They have long been sought after by cryptozoologists but, like other lake and river monsters of the British Isles, they generally remain elusive, with little evidence to suggest that they exist, except for eyewitness reports.

The horse eel is usually described as a long, serpentine creature with a mane. However, others have described it as looking more like a horse, although amphibious.

Thomas Crofton Crocker, an Irish antiquarian,

collected songs and legends of Ireland during his travels in what was then Southern Ireland in the early 1800s. One of the stories he recorded was that of the horse eel, and it is this description that is most often quoted today— that it was a wide-bodied creature with black skin and a mane.

In 1954, Georgina Carberry, a librarian, reported that she and her friends, while fishing in Lough Fadda in County Galway, spotted a creature swimming near the shore. The group reported that they could see that its long neck was raised high above the surface and it possessed a wide-open mouth full of teeth. She described the body as eel-like, but noted that, when it swam away, it had the tail of a fish.

In 1965, Captain Lionel Leslie set off an explosive charge in the water in the same area of Lough Fadda, and—to his surprise—something large surfaced and began thrashing around in the water. Sadly, nothing was actually seen clearly enough for identification, and the fish nets set across the waters remained empty of anything unusual.

Horse eel sightings date back hundreds of years. Indeed, they can be traced back to the tenth century and, in all that time, descriptions have remained extraordinarily consistent. Given this, one must ask, is the horse eel simply a huge, overgrown eel? Or maybe a new species of eel, unknown to man? Or, even more far-fetched, could it be something similar to what haunts the murky depths of Loch Ness?

But horse eels, it appears, are not the only mysterious denizens of the deep in Ireland: in September 2009, the

Express & Echo reported that Jonathan Downes, whom we have mentioned previously, spotted what appeared to be a large, moving creature in one of the lakes of Killarney, while on holiday in County Kerry, Ireland.

Along with his wife and friends, who were also carrying cameras, Downes managed to capture a vague and indefinite shape moving across the waters, while watching the lake from a nearby hill.

Downes later stated: "What we saw was a thing about nine to ten feet long. I'd love to say I saw long necks and humps and things, but I didn't. I believe it must be a large eel. It was a pale colour."

Downes's wife, Corinna, managed to take some still images of the creature from their vantage point, roughly a quarter of a mile away from the actual lake. She noted that, "It was a calm day—not much breeze or anything. All of a sudden, there were these swirls on the water. It looked like something was breaking the water on top; you could see a torpedo-like trail. We were there for a good five minutes or more. There was no sound."

Interestingly, the Downes footage came a few years after sonar readings were taken in Muckross Lake, which is roughly two hundred and fifty feet deep. Intriguingly, these findings indicated that something large *was* lurking in the water and had scientists baffled. Indeed, Pat Foley of the National Park and Wildlife Service, which oversees Killarney National Park, said that, "They were getting some sort of strange picture coming back. The image was a large and dark blob, which I presume, for economic reasons, was described as a monster."

Christened 'Muckie', the sonar images only came to light after scientists conducted a study into Arctic char, a small fish that lives in the lake. And instead of the usual small signals indicating individual fish, scientists monitoring the readings noticed something large in the water, at a depth of around ten metres—something described as being the size of a small house.

Muckross Lake itself is up to seventy metres deep, which makes it—along with its sister lake, Lough Leane—the deepest lake in Ireland. It has good fish populations, including the aforementioned Arctic char, as well as trout and Atlantic salmon, so whatever it is that is hiding in the depths, it surely would have no shortage of food. Whatever the case, the next creature from Wales is equally enigmatic.

The Afanc is a lake monster from Welsh mythology and is sometimes described as taking the form of a crocodile, giant beaver or dwarf. It is also said to be a demonic creature that will attack and devour anyone who enters its waters. Numerous versions of the tale are known to have existed, including one where the wild throes of the Afanc caused flooding, which drowned everyone in Britain except for two men, Dwyfan and Dwyfach. Another tale tells how a maiden tamed the Afanc by letting it sleep in her lap, which allowed her fellow villagers to capture it. Tragically, when the Afanc awoke, the maiden was crushed to death.

Later legends tell of King Arthur slaying the monster,

and near Llyn Barfog is a rock with a hoofprint carved into it, along with the words *Carn March Arthur* (stone of Arthur's horse), supposedly made when his steed dragged the Afanc from the deep.

Whereas the Afanc is most obviously a creature of mythology, one must wonder where the original story came from and whether or not there was a grain of truth in it all. Is it possible that the Afanc is simply a long forgotten folk memory of a 'real' lake monster (like the Loch Ness Monster), or perhaps a remnant memory of a dragon?

But the Afanc, although not really considered a water deity or a water spirit, is not the only mystical monster-like creature that the Celts believed in. The kelpie, a supernatural water horse from Celtic folklore was believed to haunt the rivers and lochs of Scotland and Ireland and appeared as a powerful horse with a black hide and a constantly dripping mane. Its skin was said to be like that of a seal, smooth yet cold to touch. Not only that, kelpies were also known to transform into beautiful women to lure men to their death.

Of course, being folklore, the story of the kelpie differs depending on the region where it is told. Other versions of the story describe the kelpie as green with a black mane, and a tail that curves over its back like a wheel and that—even in human form—is always dripping wet or has waterweed in its hair.

The water horse, a common form of kelpie, was said to lure humans, especially children, into the water to drown and eat them. It would do this by encouraging the victim to ride on its back; once in the water, its skin would become adhesive and the person stuck, wherein the creature would drag the person into the waters and drown them before devouring them—all except the heart and liver, strangely. Another form of the kelpie is that of a hairy humanoid, who would emerge from the riverside vegetation to attack passing travellers, crushing the life out of anyone unfortunate enough to be attacked.

The kelpie is thought to mainly inhabit rivers throughout Scotland, and one is recorded as being banished by St Columba from the River Ness, which could be the early inspiration for the Loch Ness Monster. Another kelpie was said to live in River Conon in Perthshire.

However, as fierce and aggressive as they are, the kelpie *can* be defeated, as its power was said to be held in its bridle, and anybody who could claim possession of it could force the kelpie to submit to their will. And a defeated kelpie was highly prized, given that it had the strength of at least ten horses and the endurance of many more. Having said that, folklore creatures have always been said to be dangerous to keep as captives or slaves. It was said that the MacGregor clan were in possession of a kelpie's bridle which had been acquired when one of the clan managed to save himself from a kelpie near Loch Slochd.

According to James Mackinley in *Folklore of Scottish Lochs and Springs,* published in 1893: "Water-horses were not always malignant in disposition. On one occasion an Aberdeenshire farmer went with his own horse to a mill to fetch home some sacks of meal. He left the horse at the door of the mill and went in to bring out the sacks. The beast, finding itself free, started for home. When the farmer reappeared and found the creature gone, he was much disconcerted, and uttered the wish that he might get any kind of horse to carry his sacks even though it were a water-kelpy. To his surprise, a water-horse immediately appeared! It quietly allowed itself to be loaded with the meal, and accompanied the farmer to his home. On reaching the house he tied the horse to an old harrow till he should get the sacks taken into the house. When he returned to stable the animal that had done him the good turn, horse and harrow were away, and he heard the beast plunging not far off in a deep pool in the Don."

In Orkney, a place we have already noted, a similar creature that lived in waterways was called the *Nuggle*, and in Shetland, the *Njogel*, or the *Tangi*. On the Isle of Man, it is known as the *Cabbyl-ushtey,* which is Manx-Gaelic for water horse. In Wales, a similar waterborne creature is known as the *Ceffyl Dwr*. Another similar Scottish water horse is the *Each Uisge,* which also appears in Ireland.

Given this array of water-dwelling spirit horses. there appears little wonder as to why many lochs, lakes, rivers and waterways in the British Isles are considered to be haunted by a river monster or, at the very least, a water serpent of some kind. And as an indication of how deep these folklore stories go, in JK Rowling's *Harry Potter and the Goblet of Fire*, Harry and his friends are almost killed by less-than-friendly mermaids in the Black Lake.

Whereas JK Rowling's mermaids are stuff of fiction, what of the accounts from Llyn Tegid, or Bala Lake, Wales's largest lake? Bala Lake itself is nearly four miles long and lies in a rift valley running northeast to southwest. It is shallow in comparison to Scottish lochs, at only forty-odd metres in depth, but covers an area of 1,084 acres. And, according to legend, the Llyn Tegid is inhabited by a monster akin to the Loch Ness Monster, known affectionately as Teggie, who has been reported since the 1920s.

Dowie Bowen, the former lake warden, saw something strange on the lake while walking along the shoreline one day: "I was looking out at the lake and saw this thing coming towards the shore. It was at least eight feet long, similar to a crocodile, with its front and rear ends about four inches above the water."

Then, in 1979, the *Sunday Express* reported that Anne Jones was gazing out on serene waters when the surface began to foam and bubble, as if boiling. For a few seconds, she saw what looked like a huge hump-backed beast: "I shall never forget it. All I saw was its huge back and froth boiling around it."

In the same year John Rowlands, a local businessman, was fishing in the lake with his cousin when they saw something they described as having a large head like a football, big eyes, and nearly eight feet long. It swam towards them and then disappeared within a few yards of the boat. Curiously, Rowlands said he wouldn't describe it as a monster, just something very large.

Another account of the monster was recorded by a B. Vickers, who encountered the creature in the summer of 1992, when he was fourteen years old. Vickers stated: "It was twilight and I was on the shingle beach of the lake, in front of the Catamaran Club, looking for flat stones to skim on the lake's calm surface. Without thinking, I suddenly turned a full 180 degrees and looked straight at the monster. The reason for my sudden turnaround was because it was looking right at me. It was about twenty metres away, its black head and neck clear above the surface of the water. The instant I saw it, it ducked under. My first thought was that a diver was playing a hoax, swimming under the surface with a Loch Ness Monster head. I immediately disregarded this for two reasons. The head had ducked under the water extremely quickly—only an animal with fins or paddles could have ducked under the surface that fast. Furthermore, there were no telltale bubbles indicating the presence of an artificial underwater breathing system. It looked to me like a plesiosaur, and I would estimate its length to be approximately twelve feet."

In March 1995, Paul and Andrew Delaney were fishing from a small boat on the lake. Both were from London and were completely unaware of the creature's supposed existence when they were surprised to see a small head appear on the surface of the lake, only twenty-five metres of so from their position. It then proceeded to raise itself on its long slender neck until it was about ten feet above the surface, before disappearing under the water.

In the very same year, a Japanese TV crew visited

North Wales to investigate the reports of the creature. The deepest area investigated was in the centre of the lake and over thirty metres in depth, but visibility made visual searching impractical, and most of the work was carried out by the mini-sub's sonar which, surprisingly, obtained a sonar trace of a very large unidentified object moving swiftly under the water. However, the crew came away empty-handed in regard to any footage.

In another report, a windsurfer recently reported being "lifted out of the water", and many boating accidents have been attributed to the creature. Monsters usually make good public relations and are good for tourism, so no one could be critical of the locals if they played up the legend to an extent. Having said that, the lake's selling point is its water sports, such as kayaking, canoeing, sailing, windsurfing and fishing. And who would want to be eaten by some giant prehistoric beast while on holiday?

A number of fanciful explanations for the monster sightings have been put forward, including one from the First World War: secret military experiments were said to have been carried out with seals, which were allegedly trained to place limpet mines on enemy ships. Of these, it is said that some escaped, and Teggie is simply one of these escapee seals. Others believe that Teggie is actually the Pontrhydfendigaid witch, Mari Berllan Biter, who, it is said, can transform herself into all kinds of shapes and forms.

Or is it possible that Teggie, just like the aforementioned 'Roch Ness Monster', is just a huge pike? And, as the locals have been known to say: "There are pike out there the size of men. If you fall in, there won't be much of you left."

Interestingly, an online forum revealed the following from one Paul Rushton who, in April 2013, was fishing on the lake with his son: "Attempting to cast out again we saw a large black shiny head surface where we had been casting our lures. We watched this thing glide along to surface about twenty yards out, making its way to the shore. We watched it for about twenty seconds until it disappeared under the surface. The head was about two and a half feet long, with about two feet sticking above the surface. It was about two metres in length. I believe that our constant casting in and out must have brought this thing up to see what was going on. We have been pike fishing [in] Bala Lake for over twenty-five years and have never witnessed anything like this. We have seen all types of birds and mammals, so what we saw was not any of those."

The legend of Teggie, like Nessie, Morag and Windermere's Bownessie, refuses to die. However, whereas the numerous lake monsters of the British Isles appear to be of the flesh-and-blood variety, our next creatures may not *quite* fall into that category.

Chapter Three

Fairies, Imps, and Other Mythical Creatures

It is a cool morning and I'm standing on the side of a rough, tarred lane, some five miles from Alfriston in East Sussex. The sun is still low on the horizon, and a cool, fresh breeze is blowing in from the south. In front of me, not one hundred metres away, is the truly breathtaking Long Man of Wilmington: a sixty-nine-metre-tall chalk figure cut into the steep grassy slope of Windover Hill.

A Scheduled Ancient Monument, the origins of the *Long Man* are unknown, although archaeological work suggests that it could date from the sixteenth or seventeenth century. But this is not the only magnificent hill figure in this picturesque part of the country, for not far away is the beautiful *Litlington White Horse*, carved onto the side of Hindover Hill and looking east over the River Cuckmere. Interestingly, there are actually two white horses on the hill, although one can no longer be seen as it was overgrown in the 1920s. The second horse, which is visible today, was cut in 1924, when three men decided to cut it overnight so as to startle the locals with the sudden appearance of the horse in the morning. Since its initial cutting, the horse has been acquired by the National Trust and has been scoured several times, although it—like many other chalk figures in Second World War—was camouflaged so as not to provide a landmark for German bombers.

Fairies, it has been said, used to live in the area just to the northeast of Alfriston, at a place called Burlough

Castle, a natural feature on the River Cuckmere. Although called a 'castle', the top has been ploughed so often that it is now nearly flat, so that any remnants or theories about the place being a medieval fort have long disappeared.

There exists a quaint local folklore story about two men who were ploughing the area when they heard a fairy from under the ground. The fairy explained that he had been baking and had broken his peel, a shovel-like tool used by bakers to slide loaves of bread and other baked goods into and out of an oven. One of the men took pity on the fairy and mended the broken peel and was later rewarded with some fairy beer. The other man refused to believe in fairies and soon died.

But fairies and fairy sightings are certainly not unusual. Indeed, no less than Sir Arthur Conan Doyle believed in their existence as, in 1920, a series of five remarkable photos appeared to show fairies cavorting and playing in an English garden. These were subsequently published in *The Strand* magazine, and Conan Doyle, a spiritualist, was over-enthusiastic and interpreted them as tangible evidence of the existence of psychic phenomena and the supernatural.

The photos were taken by sixteen-year-old Elsie Wright and ten-year-old Frances Griffiths, with the first being taken in 1917. They seem to show a variety of fairies and a winged gnome, often in conjunction with the girls themselves. The two girls regularly played together beside a stream at the bottom of a garden and would often come home with wet feet and shoes, claiming that they'd been playing with the fairies. To prove it, Elsie took her father's camera, returning half an hour later with the camera and the evidence.

Elsie's father was a keen amateur photographer and quickly developed the plate, which curiously showed Frances leaning on a bush while four fairies danced in front of her. Knowing his daughter's artistic ability, Arthur quickly dismissed the photograph as cardboard cutouts. However, not to be outdone, two months later the girls borrowed the camera again, this time returning with a photograph of Elsie seemingly playing with a twelve-inch-tall winged gnome.

Although Arthur could not explain the second photograph, he still concluded that it was a hoax and refused to lend the camera to the girls again. His wife Polly, however, believed the photographs to be genuine and, after attending a meeting of the Theosophical Society in Bradford, showed the photographs to the speaker, who promptly put them on display at the society's annual conference.

The strange photos soon came to the attention of Edward Gardner, a leading member of the society, and he had the plates examined for forgery by a photography expert who, somewhat surprisingly, gave the opinion that they were "entirely genuine, unfaked photographs [with] no trace whatsoever of studio work involving card or paper models". However, it must be noted that at no stage did he say that they were photographs of actual fairies but concluded that "these are straight forward photographs of whatever was in front of the camera at the time."

Gardner took this as a clarification that the photographs were genuine, which soon led to Conan Doyle becoming involved. Gardner and Conan Doyle then sought a second expert opinion from the photography company Kodak who agreed that the plates showed no signs of being faked. They also expressed the opinion that they were not conclusive evidence as to the existence of fairies.

In the end Kodak refused to issue a certificate of authenticity, but this didn't deter Conan Doyle who, although involved in a world tour, extolled their virtues.

Then, in 1920, Elsie took another three photographs. The first showed Frances in profile with a winged fairy; the second depicted Elsie with a hovering fairy offering her flowers; the third portrayed a strange fairy sunbath, complete with two apparently semi-transparent fairies.

Although curiosity in the Cottingley Fairies declined in the early 1920s, a newspaper reporter tracked down Elsie in 1971. In the subsequent interview, Elsie steadfastly claimed that she had taken photos of her imagination, a story she was to stick to until 1983, when the two women admitted that the photos were faked, Elsie, having copied the fairies from a popular children's book called *Princess Mary's Gift Book*. Remarkably, both maintained that, although the pictures were faked, they really had seen fairies.

Interestingly, Frances went to her death maintaining that the fifth photograph was indeed real, and that she had actually photographed fairies. Elsie disagreed and claimed that she, Elsie, had faked this one as well and that *she* was the photographer, and not Frances. "The joke was only meant to last two hours," said Elsie, towards the end of her life. "It lasted seventy years."

Although crude compared to today's digitally enhanced photographs, the girls' shots seem quite delightfully playful, if not somewhat wooden. And of course, although the photos were faked, looking back at the lovely images one gets the feeling that, fake as they are, the fairies were very much real to the girls.

Strangely though, sightings of fairies are really not that uncommon across the British Isles. In fact, so common are the reports that one could ask whether the modern-day sightings of fairies are in fact misidentified sightings of other small, human-like creatures such as elves, goblins, piskies, brownies and Knockers? Of course, this notion is simply too outlandish to even consider, but if we were to consider it then what, exactly, would we be talking about?

What *are* fairies? And what is the difference between all these strange little folk of legend? Indeed, one could even ask, what is the difference between fairies and other supernatural phenomena such as ghosts, orbs, will-o'-the-wisps, sprites and other fleetingly seen creatures or beings? Given this, maybe one should refrain from trying to find differences and should instead concentrate on the similarities, which are closer than people may think.

The English word *fairy* is a derivative of the old French word *faerie*, from the Latin *fata,* meaning fate. This means that the origins of fairies are with classical

Greek 'Fates', who were believed to control the future and destiny of humans.

Most writers of the modern age see fairies and related creatures as mythology and legend, and therefore the phenomenon is relegated to the realms of folklore. However, this appears *not* to be the case: a number of books have been written that chronicle reports of fairy encounters and, surprisingly, show a consistency from both historical and modern reports.

Sadly, the word *fairy*—or *faerie*— has been so misappropriated that it now appears to describe cute little Disney characters that twinkle and sparkle and buzz around like happy miniature humans. And yet, before they were demonised by the Christian Church, fairies were believed to be very powerful creatures and were widely feared and revered. Interestingly it has been suggested that that the medical term *stroke* comes from the Old English to be 'fairy struck'.

As such, it seems our little fairies are not the cute and harmless creatures we see in children's cartoons. Indeed, in the movie *Labyrinth,* starring David Bowie and utilising the brilliance of Jim Henson's Muppet Shop, fairies are depicted as nasty little biting creatures that are routinely killed by a goblin with an insecticide spray of some sort.

However, the notion that twenty-first century life can be shared with magical beings seems quite ridiculous, until it is realised that fairies go back beyond the written word and are found in almost all archaic cultures.

Although almost killed off in the Christian Middle Ages, the belief in fairies never quite died and made a surprising comeback during Victorian times. This is evident by the enthusiasm shown by Conan Doyle with the Cottingley Fairies and through the work of folklorists of the time, who collected stories and experiences and contributed to a growing awareness that these old beliefs were fading and being slowly lost to a rapidly modernising society.

Since that time, enthusiasts in the field of fairy lore have taken two distinct paths: the first, where the subject matter is looked at as a part of the cultural heritage and folklore, wherein old traditions and stories are examined to find meaning and norms in ancient societies; and the other, where, inexplicably, fairy encounters are reported as real events.

As we have already discovered, there are many creatures that could be attributed to fairy lore. As such, we would be wrong to simply think of fairies as a Disney construct or as Elsie Wright and Frances Griffiths portrayed them. In fact, to understand it more we need to think of fairies as a part of a greater supernatural issue that includes ghosts, religious visions, shamanism, angels, and other strange phenomena. Indeed, we should not try to prove the objective reality of fairies so much as to acknowledge that something, whatever that may be, is happening and that we really don't understand it, whether from a psychological, spiritual, cultural or physiological point of view. And this something that is happening is remarkably widespread and consistent and has been for hundreds, if not thousands, of years.

It is almost universal, due once again to the Disney-style fairy, that they are seen as an embodiment of good, whereas, as Janet Bord in her 1997 book *Fairies, Encounters with Little People* notes: "They are mostly not the pretty winged fairies that appear in children's picture books. Real fairies can be frightening."

Indeed, despite their gentle reputation, they are not all flower rings and pixie dust. Recent claimed sightings suggest they can be aggressive, bad-tempered and out to do people harm, as revealed in the first fairy census for sixty years, which heard from an incredible 450 people having reported seeing or interacting with them.

In the census, conducted by the Faery Investigation Society, witnesses spoke of a variety of phenomena, including small but aggressive fairies, tree monsters, and grumpy gnomes dressed somewhat like Oxford scholars.

The Faery Investigation Society—originally formed in 1927 and whose members included Lord Dowding, the Battle of Britain hero and, maybe surprisingly, Walt Disney—was recently relaunched by Dr Simon Young of the International Studies Institute in Florence, Italy, who stated: "Fairies seem to have changed. Gone are the friendly ones; now people are reporting a scarier, creepier underside."

Young further explained: "People's idea of fairies has changed, but it is odd how many have reported seeing things that resemble centuries-old legends. If you go back five hundred or six hundred years, fairies make people jump, they see them as fearsome and potentially dangerous beings. This has certainly come back."

Interesting, he also added: "I don't believe in fairies, wings and glitter, but I most certainly believe my witnesses. There is no question that something happened to these people. The question is, what?"

Indeed, an Essex teenager who replied to the census noted that, while on a camping trip, he walked around behind his tent to relieve himself, only to find that he was not alone: "When I looked down there appeared, silhouetted, a small shape with his hands on his hips. I could see it by a faint light coming through a large hole behind him in the hedgerow. I got the impression of someone very angry. This scared me and needless to say I could not do what I intended. Slowly backing away, I quickly apologised. [I] sincerely believed I had almost pissed on a wee folk."

Young, while being interviewed about the census, noted the same: "Generally speaking, the higher the hills the more malevolent fairies get. The fairies of the Highlands of Scotland, say, were intimidating. The fairies of the Hampshire or Sussex, say, were generally tamer, though they too had bad tempers if they were crossed. There you were more likely to be spun round and nipped a bit if you annoyed the fey. Death wasn't typical."

Young also noted that he believed that fairies "cover lots of different beings from flesh-eating Highland demons, to benign 'small people' in Cornwall. By some definitions they include will-o'-the-wisp as well as mermaids. There is a very varied spectrum, then.

However, I would say that the majority of folklore creatures that go by the name *fairy* are connected squarely to the landscape: a glen, a bridge, a clough, a wood, a lake or a house."

Bord, from her research, came up with roughly the same conclusion—although she tended to suggest that that fairies often appear wearing clothes made from natural materials, such as moss and leaves, and their garments are sometimes described as jerkins, hose, leggings, breeches. The colour of the clothing is most often recorded as green but also other earthy colours, such as reds and browns. Pointed caps are also often described but mainly in modern accounts. Surprisingly, and despite modern public perception of winged fairies, wings are rarely reported, and it would seem that fairies are pretty much flightless. However, it appears that they are able to disappear and reappear in another place in some magical way.

In her book, Bord concentrated on places that were identifiable and able to be visited today and used sources from a range of traditional folklore to modern firsthand sighting reports of fairies or fairy-like sightings, presenting them as direct reports of fairies and little people from all over the world.

In one account, she tells of a friend who reported seeing a winged fairy in 1947 by the sea at St David's in Pembrokeshire, one summer's day when she was five years old and walking home from the beach with her mother. They were in unspoiled countryside and close to a rocky shore when they saw, to the right of the path, hovering over a gorse bush, "a tiny, pure white creature, with wings, like the traditional Christmas tree fairy, but perhaps only an inch to an inch and a half high." Both were adamant that it was not a moth or a dragonfly, as it hovered in an upright position. Both were equally sure that what they had seen was a fairy.

Although this fairy appears to be more of a twentieth-century Disney construct, this is a sanitised view as, in traditional folklore, as well as modern reports, fairies—as we have seen—carry an air of foreboding and menace with them, and people generally feel frightened when they come across them.

Indeed, Bord notes that, far from being Tinkerbell-like entities, fairies vary greatly in height, from a few inches tall to human-sized, although the height is generally child-sized—even though they look like adults, often with beards.

Although Bord admits that none of her recorded encounters can be verified, she proposes that the large number of reported encounters—and the similarities between them—indicate that the 'little people' exist. However, where she cannot say, she offers possibilities: parallel universes in other dimensions or worlds, or, quite mundanely, underground.

Other examples detailed by Bord include a man who was relaxing in a garden in Bournemouth, Dorset, when he suddenly became "conscious of a movement on the edge of the lawn. I saw several little figures dressed in brown, peering through the bushes. In a few seconds a dozen or more small people, about two feet in height, in bright clothes and with radiant faces, ran onto the lawn, dancing hither and thither. This continued for four or five minutes. They were frightened away by a servant bringing tea."

Another man, a Mr Reynolds, recalled that when he was a boy of ten, while travelling on the top deck of a bus at Horsham in Sussex in 1948, he saw a little man walking across the lawn of a large garden in broad daylight. He described him as "no more than eighteen inches high and covered in hair. His face was bare but had a leathery look. The nose seemed sharp. Its arms seemed longer than a human being's."

More recently, in 1977, Cynthia Montefiore remembered a time when she was sitting in her garden in Somerset and she saw "a little figure, about eighteen inches tall, run from the lawn, finally disappearing under a young fir tree. The sturdily built figure seemed to be dressed in a brown one-piece suit. I was not able to see the face because it was turned away from me. I immediately jumped up to investigate the area around the fir tree, but there was no longer any sign of the gnome."

Marjorie Johnson, who became the secretary of the Faery Investigation Society, allegedly encountered an elf in her bedroom as a child and, as a result, grew up to be a committed fairy hunter. In the postwar years, she compiled a remarkable archive of sightings, including a family of gnomes in Wollaton Park who were observed apparently driving about in small racing cars. Johnson intended to publish her findings in her later years but was put off after some negative comments and ridicule in the tabloid press. As she told the *Sunday Pictorial*: "It has taken me years of study to win their friendship and discover the secrets of their sex life. But anyone who is admitted to the circle of fairy friendship is very fortunate. Through billions of years fairies have learned the secrets of universal love."

Interestingly, it appears that the Catholic Church is one organisation that does believe in fairies, as Tim Stanley found out while writing an article for *The Spectator* in January 2015. In his piece, he recalls speaking to a Catholic academic about the Fairy Investigation Society, who insisted that fairies were demonic, suggesting that: "The best thing you could do if you encounter a fairy is step on it or lay down slug pellets."

Stanley also details reports of "gnomes, a walking tree and 'a group of creatures, maybe twenty-five centimetres tall, humanoid, hairless, with spindly limbs and slightly shiny leathery skin' that 'wore nothing but Oxford commoners' gowns' (no mortarboards)".

However, as mentioned previously, fairies are not always quaint little folk, as the following cautionary tales from Lixnaw in Ireland suggests.

On the edge of the Ballynageragh bog in County Kerry, west of Ireland, lies a simple public housing dwelling that appears, to the outsider, to hold no secrets or hidden tales. However, over the past two decades, no fewer than five inhabitants of the tiny white building died suddenly in tragic and strange circumstances.

One man dozed off with a lit cigarette and died of smoke inhalation, while another hanged himself shortly after moving from the house. Yet another inhabitant died in a car accident, and a fourth was tragically stabbed to death while travelling in Wales. Then, in November 2013, neighbours found the body of sixty-two-year-old Susan Dunne in one of the cottage's bedrooms.

Dunne had moved in eighteen months earlier with her autistic teenage son, who was charged with her murder. These unsettling events, tapping into the culture of legend and supernatural belief, proved to be the last straw for local villagers, who petitioned for the house to be destroyed. Paddy Quilter, proprietor of Quilter's pub in Lixnaw, noted: "There's a lot of people who would love to have it. All this bullshit about knocking it down."

Although Quilter said that he didn't believe in ghosts, he and other locals are all too familiar with the legends and superstitions about fairies that once populated late-night tales in rural Ireland: "In the old days, they called it *piseog*," Quilter stated—*piseog* (pronounced *pi-shawg*) being a Gaelic term meaning superstition or anything supernatural. "There were a lot of piseogs and ghosts before electricity came in."

And, in this case, the word apparently pertained to the unusual and mysterious deaths of five residents of the public housing cottage, as Eddie Lenihan, a storyteller and folklorist. Suggests: "Was the house built in a place where it shouldn't be? Is there a fairy fort nearby? It might be built on a fairy path or a funeral path, which would be a problem. It'd be lunacy to be on one of those. According to the old people, if you're on a fairy path, you'll never have peace or luck in a house like that."

But the belief in fairies in Ireland goes even deeper than this. Criostoir Mac Carthaigh, an archivist at the National Folklore Collection in Dublin, suggests that industrialisation, while it weakened Ireland's belief in the fairy world, didn't completely stamp it out—with the result that many people adopted a better-safe-than-sorry attitude. For instance, many farmers continue their ancestors' habits of not ploughing certain parts of a field, as they were said to be favoured by fairies.

These beliefs stem from the Iron Age and beyond, when the country was said to be under the power of the mystical *Tuatha De Danann*, supposedly a supernatural race in Irish mythology and who were thought to represent the foremost deities of pre-Christian Gaelic Ireland. They were described as 'like gods and yet not gods', and were essentially thought of as fairy beings, though some Christians viewed them as fallen angels. Indeed, historical accounts of them, written by Christian monks, appear centuries after they had seemingly vanished from Ireland.

The *Tuatha De Danann* were authoritative, strong and warlike—and steeped in wisdom and magic. They claimed Ireland for their own, until they were defeated by the Milesians (ancestors of the modern-day Irish) around the beginning of the Iron Age. It is said that, when they were vanquished, they were forced to retreat underground to the otherworld and the many 'fairy forts' and mounds that now dot the countryside of Ireland are the entrances to their subterranean realm.

Interestingly, but not surprisingly, archaeologists have dated many of these mounds to the beginning of the Iron Age. As portals to the underground realm, as well as burial chambers and fairy dwellings, these mounds are supposedly protected by ancient magic to prevent humans from desecrating or entering the underground passageways. If the magic fails and they are destroyed, curses and misfortune will follow whomever was imprudent enough to demolish a fairy fort.

Even the trees and bushes that grow around the mounds are sacred and cutting one down or injuring it in any way can see the person responsible risk magical retribution, and even death.

For instance, in 1999, the National Roads Authority was notified that a proposed bypass in western Ireland would destroy a hawthorn bush that played an important role in fairy history. As a result, the government rerouted the highway and built a protective fence around the bush as an offering to the spirits because destroying the bush, it was believed, could result in violent fairy revenge: faulty brakes, crashing cars, and ultimately death.

In 2012 a farmer was fined for the destruction of two 'fairy forts' in Kilmurry, County Cork, which clearly illustrates that, though many people may not openly confess to a belief in fairies and the otherworld, this desire to protect 'fairy dwellings', and the fear of arousing their wrath, shows a deep-rooted belief in their existence.

Owen Driscoll, an agricultural consultant in West Cork, has worked with thousands of farmers over the years and suggests that fairy forts are sacrosanct, protected by cultural traditions entwined within Irish rural life: "I think that ninety-nine percent of farmers would be very slow to cause damage to a fairy fort or even a fairy tree," and, "I don't see any change in that with younger farmers. There is a sense that if you mess with the devil, then he may mess with you. You will still be told stories of a farmer who damaged a fort or removed a whitethorn tree and then died within a short time, or suffered some other tragedy. For an older generation, the idea that fairies existed went beyond a belief. It was considered absolute fact."

Jenny Butler is another who follows this line of thinking: "I think people are very hesitant about admitting to a belief in fairies. I have done some research into new-age beliefs and people are more comfortable admitting to a belief in angels, for example. Yet, very few farmers will remove a fairy fort."

She also suggests that people are hesitant about talking about fairies because the traditional means of dealing with them can be serious: "The myth of a changeling is common in folk traditions across Europe. In Ireland, there was a concept that fairies needed humans to maintain their bloodline, and they would swap an old fairy man for a young baby. Or, they might substitute a baby with a *stock*, which is an illusion of a baby that soon withers and dies."

Interestingly, these beliefs have continued into relatively recent times: in 1895, Michael Cleary convinced his family and the local community that his wife, Bridget, was a changeling. This was later confirmed by a traditional fairy doctor who attempted to cure her with herbs and, when this didn't work, they threatened her with fire and finally burned her to death. Previously, in 1894, it was said that two women were charged for placing a young boy on a hot shovel to try and burn the fairy out of him.

Butler, who holds a lectureship in the Study of Religions at University College Cork where she teaches modules on Western Esotericism and New Religious Movements as well as contemporary religions in the Irish context, explains: "There are also stories of changeling children being left on dung heaps overnight; the fairies would see one of their own being mistreated and would swap back the child they had taken. Another method of exposing a changeling was to do something unexpected; if the fairy noticed or made a comment, it would have revealed itself."

Most of these stories, fanciful as they may seem to the outsider, are matters of fact. The existence of fairies is taken as a recognised truth. They play games and music; they dance and they have funerals. They are seen as a part of a community that coexists with our own modern society and, on occasion, interact with us. They may be destructive or benevolent. However, in general they are somewhat indifferent to our presence. Nevertheless, one element of fairy lore remains consistent: if you interfere with their lives or their forts, they *will* exact revenge.

Whatever the case, fairies and stories of fairies continue to pop up in the media to this day, emphasising the fact that this phenomenon is not just a folktale steeped in the mists of time. Indeed, if anything, it appears to suggest that, like ghosts and other supernatural occurrences, *something* is happening.

An example of this can be seen when, over a number of years, a fifty-three-year-old university lecturer, John Hyatt, claimed to have photographed flying fairies in the Rossendale Valley in Lancashire: proof, in his view, of their existence.

Hyatt, Director of Manchester Institute for Research and Innovation in Art and Design at Manchester Metropolitan University, insisted that the photographs were genuine and that they had not been altered in any way: "It was a bit of a shock when I blew them up—I did a double take. I went out afterwards and took pictures of flies and gnats, and they just don't look the same."

In 2009, fifty-five-year-old Phyllis Bacon believed she took a photo of a fairy at the bottom of her garden in New Addington, near Croydon in South London. Bacon said that she simply clicked the camera button while talking to friends after dinner and wasn't even looking through the viewfinder at the time. And, rightly dumbfounded at what she saw, Bacon claimed she then spent months seeking a rational explanation for the strange image. However, after searching the internet for pictures of butterflies, moths and beetles that might match her photograph, she was still none the wiser.

Bacon, who denies that the photograph was faked in any way, added: "No one I've shown the photos to has come up with any plausible explanation as to what the figure is. Looking back, I think there was a fungi fairy ring in the garden at the time I took the picture, but I don't really know what to make of it all. To be honest, I don't know what it is, and I'm keen to listen to anyone's suggestions. But, until someone can tell me otherwise, I'm going to go on thinking it's a fairy."

Of course, both Bacon and Hyatt could have simply taken photos of insects, and camera angles, light and other atmospheric conditions have somehow managed to render the images fairy-like. Then again, as mentioned previously, these reports are, if not commonplace, then at least not infrequent.

But fairy sightings are not confined to the grassy fields of Ireland, nor suburban backyards of London: in Cornwall, they have their own version of pixies.

Piskies, like their cousins the fairies, are a race of 'little people' who live in the West Country of England. In appearance they are said to look like old men with wrinkled faces, small in stature, and with red hair. Like fairies, they tend to dress in earthy colours, especially green, and often use natural materials such as grass, leaves, moss and lichen.

Unlike trolls, dwarves, elves and goblins, piskies are generally cheerful little people, although they possess a mischievous and prankish streak. They will often help the elderly and infirm, yet will equally lead able-bodied travellers astray on the lonely and windswept moors of the West Country. Not surprisingly, they are often associated with ancient places of worship, such as stone circles and barrows.

Legends associated with piskies are many, with some seeing them as the souls of pagans unable to transcend into heaven. Others maintain that they are the remnants of pagan gods, banished when Christianity swept the land and, as such, are doomed to keep shrinking in size until they completely disappear. Early clergymen even suggested that piskies were the souls of unbaptised children, fated to roam the moors forever.

Apart from piskies, Cornwall possesses another strange little creature, often thought of as the equivalent of Irish leprechauns and English and Scottish brownies: the Knocker.

The tin mines of Cornwall have an ancient history that extends back beyond human memory and is lost in the mists of time. Cornish trade links with the Phoenicians and Carthaginians, predating Roman Britain, have been documented by Greek historians, and around 2,500 BC a trade in tin and copper started to grow, with these foreign traders exchanging bronze tools and gold ornaments for the rare Cornish minerals.

Fairy belief in Cornwall played a pivotal role in the foundation and development of Celtic culture and, as a result, Celtic Cornwall has countless myths and legends involving fairies, including the Knocker. These peculiar subterranean residents of Cornish mines are said to stand about two feet tall, are grizzled but not deformed, and wear tiny versions of a standard miner's garb, as well as committing random mischief, such as stealing miners' tools and food. Their name comes from the knocking on the mine walls that happens just before cave-ins which, to some miners, was seen as a warning to get out of the mine before an imminent collapse. Others, however, viewed them in a less than helpful light, suggesting that they were malevolent spirits and the knocking was the sound of them hammering at walls to *cause* the cave-ins.

Still, the overarching belief regarding Knockers is that they are the spirits of people who had died in previous accidents and, as such, are helpful in warning miners of impending danger. To give thanks for the warnings, and to avoid future peril, the miners often threw a crust of their pasties into the mines for the Knockers.

James MacKillop, in his 1998 publication, *Dictionary of Celtic Mythology*, describes the Knockers as "Cornish mine-spirits, thought to be the ghosts of the Jews who worked the mines in the eleventh and twelfth centuries. For the most, part the gnomelike Knocker is thought harmless when out of sight of humans and cannot endure the sign of the cross."

MacKillop also draws parallels with a Welsh relation to the Knocker, known colloquially as the Coblynau, who are "Welsh mine goblins, not unlike the Knockers of Cornwall. Although usually seen as quite ugly, and standing only eighteen inches high, they are perceived as being friendly and helpful [and] know where rich lodes of ore may be found."

Patricia Monaghan, in her 2008 book, *The Encyclopaedia of Celtic Mythology and Folklore,* also gives a description of these subterranean creatures, describing them as follows: "Strange knockings were sometimes heard on mineshaft walls. Nobody appeared after the unearthly rapping, for the invisible Knockers were the ghost of long dead miners ... The Knockers were not dangerous but helpful, their knocking growing louder when miners came near a rich vein of ore. They were private creatures, who did not appreciate being spied upon. One man who did so, by the name of Barker, managed to learn their Faery language sufficiently to hear them express their annoyance at his presence, and their plan to leave their Faery tools on his knee, hence the Cornish proverb 'stiff as Barker's knee'."

Could all these witnesses be mistaken? Could these people who claimed to have seen fairies or 'little people' be like those who claim to see ghosts? That is, are they simply mistaking or misinterpreting what they see, or are they subject to suggestion or atmospheric conditions that create a situation whereby a person's eyes misconstrue what they are actually seeing?

Without doubt, many sightings of fairies, goblins, gnomes, elves, or whatever are simply a trick of light or a misperception, influenced by familiarity with the subject through popular media and folklore. That is to say, fairy tales have been around for so long that they have become imprinted in our brains. For instance, who as a child has not read of fairies and goblins, or trolls that live under bridges, waiting billy goats? Who among us has not, as a child, hidden under our covers late at night while a storm rages outside and the creaking of the house becomes the footsteps of ghosts or other strange creatures?

And yet, as much as suggestion can play a part in our perception, there still remain numerous peculiar encounters that simply cannot be dismissed. What is one to make of sober, logical people suddenly coming across small men in green wandering across fields or along rural lanes? Or perfectly clear-headed people watching as little men in funny clothes wander across their lawn on bright, windless summer days?

Surely this can be equated to the situation we find when reporting ghost encounters, in that—although most can be easily dismissed for one reason or another—it still leaves a disconcerting number of reports that cannot be verified but cannot be totally dismissed. Perhaps we should leave the final word to Dr Simon Young: "I don't know what's going on. But perhaps it indicates in part that the countryside has a presence."

Whatever the case, there can be no denying the fact that the British Isles remains firmly tied to its ancient fairy lore and faith. This faith is evident in the many fairy-related place names, stories, as well as in the reverence with which they are often treated. And even if you dismiss tales of fairies, one thing is for certain: belief in these creatures in turn leads to a greater respect for the environment and for the ancient monuments of historic Britain and, in an age when so little is sacred, surely this is a good thing?

As such, who is to say that the fairies encountered at

Burlough Castle, northeast of Alfriston in Sussex, were not real or not? Perhaps, just perhaps, they *were* real?

The road that runs between Alfriston and Seaford is officially called Alfriston Road, although locals still call it *The White Way*, probably due to the chalky ground that it cuts through. Not only is it associated in a small way with fairies but it is reportedly haunted by the ghost of a white dog that belonged to a local lord who was murdered by robbers and later buried in a shallow grave. The dog appears on Midsummer's Eve every seven years and brings very bad luck to those who see it, as they will experience an accident or death.

But the lonely forests and fields of Sussex are not the only place where ghost dogs have been reported. Indeed, all across England these dark, fire-eyed harbingers of doom have been reported, from Cornwall to Scotland and everywhere in between. And, as we shall see in the next chapter, these devil dogs not only exist in legend, but also, it would seem, in reality, if we are to take heed of the reports of numerous reliable witnesses.

Plate 1. 50 Berkeley Square, London
Once the home of George Canning, it has been the scene of
many extraordinary deaths, believed to be the result of a
strange, unidentified creature. (Photo: Brett Desmond)

Plate 2. An Abandoned Tin Mine in Cornwall
A place supposedly inhabited by Knockers, gnome-like
Cornish mine spirits who often warned miners of impending
danger. (Photo: Sandra Lawry)

**Plate 3. Is it Possible That One of These Caves on the
Cornish Coast Hides the Sea Monster Morgawr?**
(Photo: JG Montgomery)

Plate 4. The Author on a Fishing Boat off the Cornish Coast Sadly, there was no sign of the legendary Morgawr. (Photo: KW Willcox)

Plate 5. Exmoor, a Wild and Ancient Landscape Reputedly the home of the infamous Beast of Exmoor. (Photo: Sandra Lawry)

Plate 6. Highgate Cemetery in North London
Opened in 1839, it is said that a vampire haunts the gloomy
grounds. (Photo: JG Montgomery)

Plate 7. Remote Valleys in the Scottish Highlands
These valleys are said to be haunted by evil female spirits
called Boabhan Sith or the White Woman of the Highlands.
(Photo: KW Willcox)

Plate 8. The Author at Urquhart Castle Overlooking Loch Ness in 2015 (Photo: KW Willcox)

Plate 9. The Sparkling Blue Waters of Loch Ness from Urquhart Castle (Photo: JG Montgomery)

Plate 10. Loch Ness At approximately thirty-seven kilometres long and two hundred and thirty metres deep, Loch Ness is the second-deepest loch in Scotland and contains more fresh water than all the lakes in England and Wales combined. Is it possible that a large, unidentified serpent-like creature haunts its freezing depths? (Photo: JG Montgomery)

Plate 11. Boat Wake on Loch Ness
Showing how easily one could mistake the waves for humps from a monster. (Photo: JG Montgomery)

Plate 12. Merfolk as Depicted in *Brownies and Bogles*, 1888
(Source: *Project Gutenberg*)

Plate 13. A Mermaid
(From a Picture by Otto Sinding). *Sea Monsters Unmasked
and Sea Fables Explained* by Henry Lee, 1883. (Source:
Project Gutenberg)

Plate 14. Water Deities Water deities have always been respected in Celtic societies as they were believed to be able to control the essence of life itself. The natural and fluid movements of springs, rivers and lakes clearly showed the supernatural powers of the goddesses who lived in the water. (Photo: JG Montgomery)

Plate 15. *Varney the Vampire,* or *The Feast of Blood*
By Thomas Preskett Prest. Published by E Lloyd, Fleet Street. Inspiration for the Croglin Grove vampire—or not? (Source: *Project Gutenberg*)

Plate 16. Whitby Abbey, North Yorkshire
The setting for the most famous vampire novel of all time and now the so-called capital of the world for the 'Goth' subculture. Is it possible that vampires, in various guises, may just exist? (Photo: Sandra Lawry)

Plate 17. Woodchester Mansion in the Leafy Forests of Gloucestershire Known mainly for its ghostly denizens, it is said that a black devil dog haunts the winding gravel road to the building. (Photo: JG Montgomery)

Plate 18. Old Litlington White Horse Carved onto the side of Hindover Hill, looking east over the River Cuckmere in East Sussex. Tales of fairies, ghosts and a white ghost dog abound in these parts. (Photo: JG Montgomery)

Plate 19. Fairy Rings Illustration by Antoinette Inglis. Image taken from *Child Songs of Cheer* (Lothrop, Lee & Shepard Co., 1918) by Evaleen Stein. (Source: *Project Gutenberg*)

Plate 20. Mawnan Church Between 1976 and 1978 Mawnan, and especially the church, saw numerous reports of a flying human-sized figure dubbed Owlman. (Photo: Philip White. *Used with permission.*)

Plate 21. An Eagle Owl Up to two feet tall, with a wingspan of nearly six feet, could this have been mistaken for the infamous Owlman of Mawnan? (Photo: JG Montgomery)

Plate 22. Glamis Castle The ancestral home of the Lyon family since the fourteenth century, it holds numerous legends about ghostly figures and is reputed to haunted by a vampire-like figure. (Photo: Wikipedia. *Used with permission.*)

Plate 23. Spring-heeled Jack Depicted by anonymous artist on the cover of an English Penny Dreadful (c. 1890). (Photo: Wikipedia. *Used with permission.*)

Plate 24. The River Thames
Eons old and containing the secrets of ages forgotten, is it possible that the river occasionally plays host to the odd sea monster? If footage from April 2016 is to be believed, then the answer is yes. (Photo: JG Montgomery)

Chapter Four

Black Dogs and Mysterious Panthers

Stories of phantom dogs in Britain, if not quite commonplace, are at least not *uncommon*. Indeed, almost every county has its own variation, from the Black Shuck of East Anglia, the Yeth Hound of Devon, the Lean Dog of Tring, the Padfoot of Wakefield, the Gurt Dog of the Quantocks, Mauthe Dhoog of the Isle of Man, the Gwyligi of Wales and Barghest of Yorkshire, which, bizarrely, can also refer on occasions to a ghost or household elf. And, like fairies and the 'little People', it seems that phantom 'black dogs' have been witnessed too frequently in modern times to pigeonhole as simply folklore and legend, especially when one recalls that folklore and legend often have their origins in real events.

Dr Simon Sherwood, a senior lecturer in psychology and Director of the Centre for the Study of Anomalous Psychological Processes at the University of Northampton, has stated that "sightings of Black Dogs are certainly not just legendary accounts from hundreds of years ago. I still receive accounts from people who have been looking for information about similar sightings and have come across my website. I have probably collected about fifty or sixty accounts from around the world over the past ten years or so and some of these are recent sightings."

And, as in the case of fairies, there appear to be many common traits in the sightings.

In appearance, phantom dogs vary slightly from region

112

to region. However, it is not unusual for them to be described as being very large, with blazing red eyes and a shaggy coat. Phantom dogs are not always black, as is the case of the dog near Alfriston. Indeed, the ghost dog that is supposed to haunt the area around Cawthorpe and Haugham in Lincolnshire is also described as white. Strangely, the Cu Sith, the traditional fairy/ghost dog of Scotland, is dark green in colour and has a shaggy tail.

More often than not, black dogs are associated with a specific location such as an old road, track or lane, as is the case for the Black dog that haunts the rough gravel lane to Woodchester Mansion in Gloucestershire. Indeed, if one is to look around, one will find many an English lane named after a phantom hound, such as Black Dog Walk in Crawley, West Sussex, and Black Dog Way in Gloucester. Whether or not these names relate to ancient legends of black devil dogs is debatable, but, as so many Blackberry Ways are related to archaic blackberry patches, maybe it is so in this case as well.

In many local traditions a sighting of a black dog is regarded as a portent of death or doom, especially those seen in ancient churchyards. And, so it was to be on the morning of Sunday 4 August 1577, when a violent and destructive storm darkened the skies over Bungay in Suffolk. As the storm raged overhead, the parishioners were suddenly confronted with the sight of a black dog, which, as if by magic, appeared in the church during a service. Two people died instantly when it ran past them and another was severely burned. Today, a weather vane in the town depicts a black dog and a flash of lightning.

Meanwhile, in Blythburgh, some ten kilometres away, another black dog appeared in the parish church and struck three people dead, as well as leaving scorch marks on the front door.

Although these two examples suggest weather-related phenomena such as some form of ball lighting (which could certainly burn someone if they were close enough, and could possibly kill a person if they touched it), it is difficult to make any definitive judgement, given the period of time that has passed since the event. After all, how could people mistake a ball of glowing light for a large dog?

In the seventeenth century Richard Cabell, a local squire at Buckfastleigh, was reputed to have sold his soul to the devil. Described as having a passion for hunting and cruelty, he was also rumoured to have murdered his wife. With his death in 1677, he was interred, but on the night of his internment a phantom pack of hounds came loping across the moor to howl at his tomb. From that night, on every anniversary of his death, he could be seen leading the phantom pack across the moor. Often, the pack of ghostly hounds could be found around his grave, howling and yelping. The villagers were quite concerned about these ghostly goings-on and, in an attempt to lay his soul to rest, constructed a building around the tomb. Then, just to make certain, they placed a huge slab of rock on top of the grave. With this, the sightings of the ghostly Cabell and his hellish pack of hounds ceased.

Given this, not all phantom dogs are bringers of death and bad luck, some being quite benevolent at times.

Augustus Hare, whom we shall visit later in the book in relation to the Croglin vampire, recalls a tale (in his book, *In My Solitary Life*) about a man called Greenwood from Swancliffe, who had to ride for a mile through a wood, in darkness, to reach his destination. As he entered the woods, he was joined by a huge black dog that pattered alongside him until he emerged from the trees, where it promptly and mysteriously disappeared.

On the return journey, he was again surprised when the dog reappeared and once again mysteriously disappeared. It emerged, some years later, that two prisoners about to be hanged confessed that they were going to rob and murder Greenwood that night in the wood, but the presence of a large black dog had stopped them.

These ghostly black dogs most often seem to haunt ancient places, laneways, forest tracks, crossroads, old churchyards and prehistoric sites. Many of these places are associated with local supernatural tales and superstitions and appear to be a point between worlds: that is, the real and tangible world in which we live, and the less tangible world of the paranormal. Strangely, many black dog haunts are said to be on ley lines, alleged alignments of geographical places such as ancient monuments and megaliths, natural ridge-tops and water features which suggests that the apparitions represent, or use some sort of natural earth energy to exist. Indeed, it does appear that certain geophysical features may affect the human mind and, as such, could possibly lead us to imagine that we have seen something strange or unworldly. On the other hand, maybe these creatures do exist, a throwback to earlier times when man was not much more than an articulate ape, and our survival senses were much heightened in comparison to modern times.

In medieval times crossroads were seen as places of evil, for here the spirits wandered aimlessly, wondering which way to go to get back to their former earthly abode. And it was places such as crossroads where gallows were often sited: one, so that any traveller passing the crossroads could see what happened to criminals in this area; and two, as we have seen, to confuse the spirit or ghost of the dead person when they attempted to return to their living abode.

Not surprisingly, then, crossroads and gallows sites are places where black dogs are often witnessed. Tring, in Hertfordshire, is one such place. In 1751, an old woman was unjustly drowned for allegedly practising witchcraft, and a local chimney sweep was held responsible for the death. Subsequently, he was hanged and gibbeted, and many a sighting of a large, shaggy dog with flaming eyes and long teeth have since been attributed to the death. Interestingly, especially if we recall the Bungay and Blythburgh sightings of 1577, flames and scorched earth are quite often associated with black dog sightings.

There are probably innumerable explanations for modern-day sightings, as the phantom black dog is a powerful standard, now well ensconced into modern stories such as the *Hound of the Baskervilles* by Arthur Conan Doyle. However, this is not to say that people do not witness these creatures.

In recent years, more and more reports have continued to emerge of black dogs roaming the country. So many, in fact, that certain zoologists and experts in the paranormal are calling for an investigation to prove or disprove their existence. Richard Freeman, zoological director at the Centre for Fortean Zoology, has noted that black dogs have been reported in Britain, across Europe, and in South America, and that he "would welcome support for a thorough investigation into their existence. If one could be captured on film or filmed with a thermal camera it might give us a clue to the nature of these creatures."

However, as frequent as contemporary sightings are, the first English account of a black dog probably appeared in the *Anglo-Saxon Chronicle* in 1127: " Let no one be surprised at the truth of what we are about to relate, for it was common knowledge throughout the whole country that immediately after his arrival [Abbot Henry of Poitou at Abbey of Peterborough]—it was the Sunday when they sing Exurge Quare o, D—many men both saw and heard a great number of huntsmen hunting. The huntsmen were black, huge and hideous, and rode on black horses and on black he-goats and their hounds were jet black with eyes like saucers and horrible. This was seen in the very deer park of the town of Peterborough and in all the woods that stretch from that same town to Stamford, and in the night the monks heard them sounding and winding their horns. Reliable witnesses who kept watch in the night declared that there might well have been as many as twenty or thirty of them winding their horns as near they could tell. This was seen and heard from the time of his arrival all through Lent and right up to Easter."

But whereas the previous report could be put down to medieval superstition, in 1908 the following was recorded in the *Journal of the Society for Psychical Research* after an investigation of strange animal apparitions, which had been reported in a lane in a village situated approximately halfway between London and Bristol. The apparitions were believed to be the spirit of a local farmer who had hanged himself in an outhouse about a century earlier.

One of the villagers gave the following account: "In the beginning of January, 1905, about half past seven in the evening, I was walking up from the Halfway [a local inn]. I suddenly saw an animal that seemed to be like a large, black dog appear quite suddenly out of the hedge and run across the road quite close in front of me; I thought it was the dog belonging to the curate. I was just going to call it to send it home, when it suddenly changed its shape, and turned into a black donkey standing on its hind legs. This creature had two glowing eyes, which appeared to me to be almost as big as saucers. I looked at it in astonishment for a minute or so, when it suddenly vanished."

Another case, this time involving a four-year-old girl who had been evacuated from London during World War II, has also been widely reported: "My encounter took place one late afternoon in summer, when I had been sent to bed but was far from sleepy. I was sitting at the end of the big brass bedstead, playing with the ornamental knobs and looking out of the window, when I was aware of a scratching noise, and an enormous black dog had walked from the direction of the fireplace on my left. It passed round the end of the bed, between me and the window, round the other corner of the bed, towards the door. As the dog passed between me and the window, it swung its head round to stare at me—it had very large, very red eyes, which glowed from inside as if lit up, and as it looked at me, I was quite terrified, and very much aware of the creature's breath, which was warm and strong as a gust of wind. The animal must have been very tall, as I was sitting on the old-fashioned bedstead, which was quite high, and our eyes were level. Funnily enough, by the time it reached the door it had vanished. I assure you that I was wide awake at the time and sat for quite some long time wondering about what I had seen, and to be truthful, too scared to get into bed, under the covers, and go to sleep. I clearly remember my mother and our host, sitting in the garden in the late sun, talking, and hearing the ringing of the bell on the weekly fried-fish van from Birmingham as it went through the village! I am sure I was not dreaming, and have never forgotten the experience, remembering to the last detail how I felt, what the dog looked like, etc."

Simon Sherwood also relates a story that happened to him as a small child, between the ages of three and five, while living in Spalding, Lincolnshire:

"The year was about 1974. I had been in bed a couple of hours. I awoke to hear a pattering of feet. I looked up, thinking it was my dog, but to my terror I saw a massive black animal, probably with horns, but perhaps ears, galloping along the landing towards my bedroom. I tried to scream, but I found it impossible. The creature's eyes were bright yellow and as big as saucers. The animal got to my bedroom door and then vanished as quick as it has appeared. I then managed to scream and my mum came in to calm me down. She said it was a reflection of car headlights, what I thought was a ghost. I believed this until a few years later when I was reading a local paper, which had an article about a haunted council house which was inhabited by a poltergeist. A variety of objects were hurled at the family's baby child. The father claimed that a black dog rushed at him and then disappeared. He also claimed that a black goat had been seen running around the house. I also thought I saw a ghostly black goat on the landing of my old house. After reading this article, I was convinced that what I thought had happened a few years back had most probably happened."

Remarkably, Sherwood noted that he found it difficult to recall a visual image of the 'apparition', which he estimates to have been between two and a half to three feet high, with its fur standing on end and seemingly snarling or at least it was baring its teeth.

Whereas Sherwood may have not been able to recall the image of his black dog sighting, the following report, which appeared in *English Fairy and Other Folk Tales* by Edwin Sidney Hartland in 1890 leaves no doubt as to what was experienced in a village near Aylesbury, in Buckinghamshire:

"This man was accustomed to go every morning and night to milk his cows in a field, which was some distance from the village. To shorten his walk, he often crossed over a neighbour's field, and passed through a gap in the hedge; but one night, on approaching the gap, he found it occupied by a large, black, fierce-looking dog. He paused to examine the animal, and as he looked at him his fiery eyes grew larger and fiercer, and he had altogether such a fiend-like and 'unkind' appearance that he doubted whether he was 'a dog or the bad spirit'. Whichever he was, he thought he would be no pleasant antagonist to encounter. So, he turned aside and passed through a gate at the end of the field. Night after night he found the same dog in the gap, and turned aside in the same manner. One night, having fallen in with a companion, he returned homeward with him across his neighbour's field, being determined, if he found the dog in the gap, to make an attack upon him and drive him away. On reaching the gap there stood the dog, looking even fiercer and bigger than ever. But the milkman, wishing to appear valiant before his companion, put down his milk-pails, which were suspended from a yoke across his shoulders, and, attempting to speak very bravely, though trembling all over, he exclaimed: 'Now, you black fiend, I'll try what ye're made of!' He raised his yoke in both his hands, and struck at the dog with all his might. The dog vanished, and the milkman fell, senseless, to the ground. He was carried home alive, but remained speechless and paralytic to the end of his days."

And, in this case, we see the black dog not just as a flesh-and-blood creature of immense size, but also possessing a supernatural ability to not only disappear but to hex the witness in question. And, as we have previously read, it appears that black dogs straddle the murky world between superstition and what we see as reality, something we shall see further as we examine more reports of the creatures.

And so it was for our next report, which happened in the summer of 2001 as night was setting on the A684 between Northallerton and Leeming Bar in Yorkshire, when two women witnessed a huge black dog that ran in front of their car. The driver closed her eyes and braked hard, expecting to hit the creature, while the passenger watched the hound *pass through* the bonnet unharmed, noticing that, bizarrely, the creature had no facial features, had floppy ears, and was shadow-like.

Other remarkable sightings of black dogs have been reported in Cannock Chase in Staffordshire, an area that seems to attract strange phenomena, which we will examine further in later chapters. However, at present, it is black dogs that we seek—and Cannock Chase is certainly an area where they have been regularly reported.

The *Birmingham Mail* of 17 March 2009 recorded: "Reports have been received on paranormal websites of the demonic dog roaming our area. The hound, also known as the 'ghost dog of Brereton', has been seen on numerous occasions stalking the roads leading into Brereton. The apparition has been described as large, black, muscular, with sharp pointed ears and strangely glowing eyes. British folklore indicates that the black dog forewarns death."

The most prominent of these black dog sightings occurred in the 1970s and early 1980s. Nigel Lea, while driving through the Chase in 1972, described seeing a ball of light crash into the ground. According to his account, he slowed down to take a closer look and was confronted by "the biggest bloody dog [he had] ever seen".

Apparently jet-black and extremely muscular, with huge paws and pointed ears, the animals stared at him for twenty to thirty seconds before slinking off into the trees, never at any stage taking its eyes off Lea, who stated that the creature seemed to project a negative, menacing feeling. Strangely, within a month of the sighting, one of Lea's close friends died in an industrial accident, which Lea believes may be connected to the dog apparition.

In the early 1980s, more reports of the beast began to surface, including at least two occasions when it was seen by terrified witnesses on lonely stretches of road before simply vanishing into thin air.

One member of the public, Sylvia Everett, a local, wrote to the *Advertiser* about her experience: "We recalled an incident that happened in July some four or five years ago, driving home from a celebration meal at the Cedar Tree restaurant at about 11.30 p.m. We had driven up Coal Pit Lane and were just on the bends before the approach to the Holly Bush when, from a high hedge of trees on the right-hand-side of the road, the headlights picked out a misty shape, which moved across the road and into the trees opposite."

Continuing, she recalled: "We both saw it. It had no definite shape, seeming to be a ribbon of mist about eight inches to two feet in depth and perhaps nine to ten feet long, with a definite beginning and end. It was a clear, warm night, with no mist anywhere else. We were both rather stunned, and my husband's first words were: 'My goodness, did you see that?' I remembered remarking I thought it was a ghost. Until now, we had no idea of the history of the area or any possible explanation for a haunting. Of course, this occurrence may be nothing to do with 'the ghost dog' or may even have natural explanation. However, we formed the immediate impression that what we saw was something paranormal."

But this was not the first of similar stories to be reported around the area. In 1934, Ivan Vinnel, then twelve years old, had a strange encounter in his hometown of Burntwood. With a friend, and around sunset, the pair encountered a ghostly "tall dark man", who was "accompanied by a black dog" that had materialised out of a dense hedge ten yards from their position. The man and dog walked silently by the children then vanished.

Vinnel later mentioned the strange sighting to his uncle, who confirmed that he too had seen the ghostly dog on a few occasions when he was a child and that it was always at the same location, on an old road from the village of Woodhouses to an area of Burntwood near the hospital. And, as with most black dog sightings, this creature would follow what seemed to be a set path before simply disappearing, apparently into thin air.

Then, in 2006, reports from the Chase emerged of a wolf-like creature roaming the area. Indeed, on the morning of 28 June, motorists on the M6 continued to report sightings of the greyish-black creature, which was racing between lanes at rush hour, dodging cars before leaping over a fence into the undergrowth. Although written off as an overly large husky, a government employee later noted: "Everyone who saw it is convinced it was something more than a domestic dog. I know it sounds crazy, but these people think they have seen a wolf."

It must be noted here that wolves have been extinct in England since the late 1400s to early 1500s.

Interestingly, just a few days previous to the mass 'wolf' sightings, Jim Broadhurst and his wife had their own strange encounter, with a similar creature. He stated that he and his wife had witnessed what looked like a large wolf or a giant dog walking through the woods, about one hundred and fifty feet from their position. At one stage, the beast stopped and, as if sensing the couple watching it, looked intently at them, filling the couple with an immense sense of dread and fear. However, the creature did not attack but remarkably reared up on its hind legs and stood in the air before backing into thick trees and forest. Understandably, the couple fled and have not since returned to the woods, believing that some sort of monster exists in there. And, somewhat similar to Nigel Lea in 1972, the pair reported that they were plagued with bad luck for months after their encounter.

Later, in March 2009, the *Birmingham Mail* followed up their previous article with another on the same subject, noting that the 'ghost dog of Brereton', had been seen on numerous occasions, stalking the roads leading into Cannock and Huntington.

Reports of black dogs are remarkably similar, which either suggests that witnesses expect, by suggestion, to see a large dog with a number of supernatural-like features, or they are legitimately reporting what they have seen. Whether black dogs are flesh and blood or simply ghostly dogs is debatable, as is whether or not they bring bad luck upon all who see them, or are precursors to doom or death. Whatever the case, the black dog that haunts the forests of Cannock Chase would appear to be very real. And, as we will see in further chapters, it is not the only strange things happening in these woods.

Other supernatural devil dogs have been reported in Ailsworth in Northamptonshire, where a huge hound, possessing eyes that burn as bright as the sun, apparently tries to sneak up on people, while in Algarkirk in Lincolnshire, around the village church, a black dog was described by a witness as being tall and lean, with a long neck and a protruding muzzle. Puzzlingly, this hound is not regarded as an ill omen.

In Wiltshire, between the villages of Allington and All Cannings, is a black dog that used to frighten children in the area. One man reported being chased by the creature, while another couple who spotted the hound said it stood almost as tall as their pony. In Amlwch in Wales, a phantom hound is said to haunt a prehistoric stone circle that lies between the village and St Ellian Church. In Balsham in Cambridgeshire, on Wratting Road, a black dog has been observed, although it is believed to have a bald head and wide eyes, similar to that of a monkey, while the body is that of a large black shaggy dog. It apparently bounds out in front of cars travelling along the road, only to leap out of the way at the last possible second, either on all four legs or standing upright. In 1974, a woman passing through the Beccles Cemetery in Suffolk reported watching a large white dog as it faded away in front of her.

In summary, it appears that the phenomenon of phantom and black dogs is a multifaceted blend of folklore, alleged sightings, and local superstition which has its roots in the distant past, so distant that it is now impossible to really make any judgement upon the veracity of sightings—although, interestingly, in May 2014, in the ruins of Leiston Abbey, Suffolk, archaeologists found the bones of a dog measuring seven feet in length. The bones were discovered only a few miles from two churches where the Black Shuck is said to have killed worshippers during an almighty thunderstorm in August 1577. And, apart from that, it appears to have been buried in a shallow grave at precisely the same time as Shuck is said to have been terrorising the locals around Suffolk and the East Anglia region.

However, as numerous as sightings are, black dogs or devil dogs are not the only strange four-legged beasts that appear to haunt the forests and fields of the British Isles. Whereas the previous appear to be a blend of flesh and blood and the supernatural, the next collection of creatures could be considered real, if not a little anomalous: alien big cats.

To begin, one must point out that alien big cats are in no way associated with UFOs, little green men, and anything else to do with extraterrestrials. By labelling the large cats as alien, one is simply pointing out that they do not belong in the environment in which they have been witnessed, which is obviously the case when we are talking about the British Isles.

But before we examine this phenomenon more closely, I should point out that I have had my own perplexing alien black cat sighting—although not in the northern climes of Britain, but in Australia in the mid-1990s. Although I now forget the exact year, I was studying anthropology, archaeology, and Indigenous Australian studies as part of an Applied Science degree at university. During one of my assessments, I was required to make some observations of Indigenous landscapes in the Canberra region of Australia, and while wandering around an area of bush south of Canberra—part of a primary outdoor education centre called Birrigai, which lies on the border of Namadgi National Park—I encountered what I could only describe as a panther.

At first, I thought the creature was simply a large dog but upon closer examination, from a distance of less than one hundred metres, it was apparent that it walked like a house cat with low slung and graceful movements. I was particularly taken by its tail, which was long and held at an angle almost horizontal to the ground, very unlike a dog.

The creature was jet-black and, at the time, all I could think of was that it appeared to be an enormous black house cat, and by enormous I am talking nearly two feet tall at its shoulders, and three to four feet in length. Its tail then stretched at least another foot and a half behind it. It was, to put it simply, exactly like pictures of black panthers one would see when reading *National Geographic*. Indeed, to make another comparison, it was somewhat like Bagheera from Rudyard Kipling's *The Jungle Book*.

The creature emerged from a scrubby patch of low bushes and walked an easterly path for about forty to fifty metres before disappearing again. Although I watched in hope that it would reappear, it didn't—and the whole sighting would have taken less than thirty seconds.

Later, I examined the area where I had seen the large cat but could find absolutely no evidence of it having been there. However, the distance from where I saw the cat to where I was standing only reinforced the fact that this was an exceptionally large cat.

Sadly, in 2003 bushfires raged through Namadgi National Park and into suburban Canberra, killing four people and destroying nearly five hundred houses. The area where I had the alien big cat sighting was decimated, and not a single living tree was left standing. Today, I cannot even point out where the whole episode took place: the fire left nothing.

Having said that, at the time I was working for the Australian National Parks and Wildlife Service and reported the sighting to a ranger. Imagine my surprise when he simply nodded and told me that I wouldn't believe the number of reports he had heard concerning huge panther-like beasts in the bush south of Canberra. Indeed, he described to me how one day he was driving a four-wheel-drive vehicle in a very isolated part of the National Park when he rounded a bend and saw three or four large brown and white cats, similar to pumas, race off into the bush.

But it is not my experience that we are interested in, as, for many decades now, huge cat-like creatures have been widely reported and documented right across Britain, especially in the southwest of England. Generally, these reports tell of cats resembling black panthers or sandy-coloured pumas and lions, although, on occasion, spotted and striped large cats have also been reported.

Considering the apparent destruction these large cats are responsible for, it is surprising not more is heard about them. Mutilated cattle, half-eaten sheep, and slashed family pets are a testament to the ruthless killing efficiency of these creatures, which, now and then, leave tantalising clues as to their existence, such as felid-like prints.

As well as prints, these creatures often leave their mark in other ways, as Ron and Betty Harper from Brassknocker Hill at Claverton Down, five miles south of Bath, found to their consternation in July 1979. One day, the Harpers noticed that bark had been stripped off an oak tree at their cottage, and their goat seemed as if it had been traumatised in some way. Although squirrels *are* known to strip bark from trees, they usually strip the top of branches, whereas the damage here looked as if it had been done by an animal hanging underneath. The bark had been stripped off all the branches from twenty feet up, and the teeth marks were ten to twenty times the size of those of a squirrel.

The Harpers also noted that all the birds seemed to have disappeared and the nearby woods were silent. By August, fifty trees had been stripped, and a man driving through Monkton Combe one night reported seeing an animal three to four feet tall, with bright white rings around its eyes, like a bespectacled bear. The creature was never identified.

In March 2005, a large black cat-like creature attacked Anthony Holder, just beyond his back garden in Sydenham Park, southeast London. Holder heard his cat scream and, thinking it was being attacked by a fox or a dog, he jumped over his back fence to chase it away, only to encounter a large feline emerging from the bushes. The creature then pounced on him, knocking him over: "It scratched down the side of my face, and its teeth sank into my fingers. Its face was so close to me I could smell its breath." After about thirty seconds he was able to break away from the creature, and he later estimated its size as about six feet long and three feet tall.

Police who later attended saw a large black cat-like animal "about the size as a Labrador dog" and, while paramedics attended to Holder's injuries, armed officers conducted a search of a nearby railway line and allotments, but came up empty-handed.

In July 1963, a man in Shooters Hill, southeast London, reported seeing an enormous cat and, not long afterwards, what was described as a "large, golden animal" jumped over the bonnet of a police patrol car in the area. Before long, a hunt was organised, including 126 police with twenty-one dogs, thirty soldiers, ambulancemen, and RSPCA officials, and covering an area of 850 acres. Some seven-inch-wide paw prints were found, but no animal, which by now had been nicknamed the 'Surrey Puma'.

Police soon learned of several other sightings of large cats around Surrey since the previous winter, and with public imagination running wild, scores of alien big cats were reported across southeast England. So widespread was the panic that the day book of Godalming police station in Surrey listed an incredible 362 large cat reports between September 1964 and August 1966.

With the 'Surrey Puma' entering popular and national folklore in the 1960s, large cats in other regions were also given nicknames. In 1978 a large cat reported to be seen in Cambridgeshire was dubbed the Fen Tiger. Later, in Gwent in 1983, the Beast of Brechfa appeared, while in Cornwall the Beast of Bodmin surfaced in 1992.

Bodmin Moor is a spooky and unnerving place. Wild and rugged, the area is steeped in history and has more than its fair share of myths and legends, including Dozmary Pool, the lake into which the dying King Arthur instructed Sir Bedivere to cast Excalibur. It also contains the ghost of Charlotte Dymond, who is often seen walking in the area where she was murdered, clad in a gown and a silk bonnet.

The Beast of Bodmin is a panther-like animal that is reputed to stalk the windy and desolate climes of Bodmin

Moor in Cornwall. It is thought responsible for occasional reports of mutilated and slain livestock. It is also sometimes assumed that sightings and stories of the Beast could simply be a modern manifestation of earlier black dog legends, such as those that inspired Conan Doyle's *The Hound of the Baskervilles.*

But could such a beast exist? Unlike alien big cats reported in countries such as Australia, it seems that there is less chance the creature could exist, due in the main to the improbably large numbers of cats that would be necessary to maintain a breeding population, and because climate and food-supply issues would make the existence of such a creature unlikely.

There exists a reasonably plausible theory that British big cats, such as the Beast of Bodmin, could have quite possibly been imported as part of a private collections or zoos and later escaped or were set free. Given that it is illegal to own or import a big cat, the owner would have no reason to report it if it were missing or were set free. However, an official investigation conducted by the Ministry of Agriculture, Fisheries and Food in 1995 found that there was no verifiable evidence of exotic felines running wild in Britain and that the savaged farm animals were probably the result of an indigenous species. Interestingly, I wonder what sort of indigenous creature can rip a cow to pieces, given that wolves have long been considered extinct in Britain, and badgers are not quite large enough to do any real damage.

Just after the release of the government report, a boy walking along the River Fowey found something quite incredible, and very foreign: a large cat skull. It measured about ten centimetres wide and eighteen centimetres long and, although lacking its lower jaw, possessed two prominent canines, suggesting that the skull was that of a large cat such as a panther or leopard.

The skull was quickly sent to the Natural History Museum in London for identification and, to their surprise, they found that it indeed had come from a young male leopard. However, any suggestion that it may be the Beast of Bodmin, or even one of its offspring, was quickly debunked, as it was found that the cat had not died in Britain, and that the skull had been imported as part of a leopard-skin rug. Evidence of this was in the way the back of the skull was cleanly cut off, which was consistent with a method commonly used to mount the head on a rug. In addition, inside the skull was found an egg case laid by a tropical cockroach that simply did not exist in Britain. Also, well-cut marks made by a knife were evident on the skull indicating that it had been skinned by a knife. Sadly, the skull only proved that it *wasn't* the Beast of Bodmin.

Still, even with this debunking, sightings of the elusive Beast have not abated with more than three hundred sightings in 1996 alone. And, given the huge number of sightings in 1996, it doesn't seem unusual that, in October 1997, employees of the Newquay Zoo reported to have found and identified paw prints in mud to the south of Bodmin Moor. They claimed that the prints were indeed those of a puma. Not long after this discovery, a photograph of the Beast emerged and it appeared to show a pregnant adult puma. Although the cause for much debate the photos were never authenticated. On the other hand, they were also never conclusively debunked and, as a result, the photos remain controversial to his day

But if the Beast of Bodmin is controversial, even if it appears there is some chance of it actually existing, then what of another large, unexplainable cat that is reported to roam the fields of Exmoor in Devon and Somerset?

There have been numerous reports of sightings of the Beast of Exmoor, another large and alien big cat. The Beast itself is listed in the official Exmoor National Park website under 'Traditions, Folklore, and Legends', even though sightings were first reported in the 1970s and became quite infamous in 1983 when a farmer claimed to have lost over one hundred sheep to savage attacks by a creature unknown, all in the space of three months.

The Beast itself has been described as ranging in colour from black to tan or dark grey and, as such, is generally thought to be a cougar or black leopard, possibly released sometime in the 1960s or 1970s, when a law was enacted making it illegal for large cats to be kept in captivity outside of zoos. Whereas this seems to be a reasonable theory, it must be realised that cougars and leopards generally only live for twelve to fifteen years, which means that, if a big cat was released nearly fifty years ago, then it would be well and truly dead by now. Of course, this brings up the intriguing possibility that maybe more than one cat was released, and over time they bred, thus explaining sightings to this day. Indeed, in 2006, the British Big Cats Society reported that a skull found by a Devon farmer was that of a puma.

Photographs of the Beast have been taken on a number of occasions, and all of them appear to show a large cat similar to a puma and a panther. Sadly, as with many photos concerning large unidentified animals (not just cats), there is nothing in the shots to give a true indication of the size, which leads one to suspect that the photos could just as likely be that of a large domestic cat, or in the case of blurry, long-distance shots, a dog.

Most researchers believe that the sightings are simply that of large escaped domestic cats whose size has been greatly misinterpreted or exaggerated, although how one mistakes a fat house cat for a panther is beyond me. As well, others suggest that it is simply a large dog, which would explain the attacks on livestock. And yet, even a child does not mistake a dog for a cat.

There is a theory that, as the beast seems to have both the features of a puma and a leopard, that it is in fact a hybrid. Such a hybrid has been known to exist in captivity and is called a Pumapard. Is it possible that both a puma and leopard were released on the moor and happened to find each other? However, as much as this seems like a reasonable theory, it should be noted that hybrid offspring are often stunted and short-lived as well as sterile, which rules out the creatures continually breeding to keep up the numbers needed for a breeding population.

Still, even with misinterpreted sightings and inconclusive photo evidence, the increases in livestock deaths saw a response from the Ministry of Agriculture in which Royal Marines snipers were deployed in the

Exmoor hills, ostensibly to shoot the creature if seen. However, although some Marines claimed to have fleetingly seen the Beast, no shots were fired and no animal was killed. Interestingly, during this time the number of attacks on farm animals decreased, notably only to rise again when the Marines were pulled out of the field.

Remarkably, even though there had been over two hundred reported attacks by 1987, and more in 1995 and 2001, the Ministry of Agriculture concluded that the Beast was simply a myth, a hoax, or a case of mistaken identity. However, in January 2009 a strange carcass was found washed up on a beach in North Devon, leading people to speculate whether or not this was the infamous Beast of Exmoor. Sadly, it was later revealed to be nothing more mysterious than a seal.

But while the Beast of Exmoor has been written off as a nonentity, the same cannot be said for other mysterious beasts that keep on appearing across the British Isles. For instance, in 2015 a mystery animal was spotted prowling in the garden of a house on the outskirts of Plymouth by Carole Desforges, an office worker, who saw the animal from her living room and managed to get a few snaps of it through the window before it ran away. At first, she thought it may have been a fox, but upon reviewing the pictures she changed her mind. Whereas some have suggested that the photographs show a puma or a leopard, she stated: "I don't know what it is, but people have been suggesting it could be some kind of big cat. A puma or a lynx have both been mentioned. I don't know what it is, but I have never seen anything like it before."

Interestingly, latest figures show there have been an estimated two hundred big cat sightings in Devon and Cornwall over the last thirteen years, one of which was that of a tiger, reported in Exmouth in Devon. As well, a puma was spotted in Efford by a man who called to report it to police.

Danny Bamping of the British Big Cat Society, noted: "In Britain seventy-five percent of the reports is of big black cats, but the unanswered question is what they are. There's no doubt in my mind that there could be black leopards, but possibly a hybrid of a wild and domesticated cat."

But it's not just southwest England that receives reports of these creatures: in 2004, in Antrim in Ireland, the Ulster Society for the Prevention of Cruelty to Animals (USPCA) suggested that a black panther was living near the village of Ballybogey, outside Portrush, and a brown-coloured puma was roaming the hills near Ballycastle. As a result, an operation jointly run by the USPCA and the police was conducted to attempt to catch the creature. However, it was unsuccessful.

The first sightings of the cat were reported in early August in the Portrush, Portballintrae; in Bushmills area, a few days later, paw prints found in the area were identified as being made by a mountain lion, possibly a puma or panther. In August, a farmer in the Bushmills area blamed the cat for killing a ram when it attacked a flock of sheep.

And, as recently as May 2016, the *Daily Mail* reported that a couple, while driving through the English countryside, claimed to have encountered a black panther. Robert Ingram and his wife Nicola encountered the frightening creature while driving through Croome Court, a National Trust property, at 1.00 a.m. and claim that it was as tall as their car window. He noted, "It was petrifying. It looked like it was on steroids. We were driving along outside the National Trust property. There are lots of open fields around there, when suddenly I spotted something in the road ahead. It was getting dark, but I saw its eyes reflect in my headlights. We stopped the car, and it was just standing there. We'd heard rumours about an escaped panther in the area, but we'd thought it was a load of nonsense—but when I saw this animal with my own eyes, I was stunned. It was enormous, far too big for a fox or a dog. It must have weighed about nine stone, about the same as a slim adult. It looked right at us and walked up to the car. It then lowered the front of its body and looked like it was going to pounce."

Maybe not surprisingly, given the previous reports, alien big cats seem to turn up regularly in the English countryside. In September 2006, the *Frome & Somerset Standard* published a report about a big cat that was sighted one night in Victoria Park in Frome in Somerset, at the eastern end of the Mendip Hills, a place we shall examine in a later chapter.

The Badcox Beast, as it was dubbed, was seen on two consecutive evenings by two park staff, the first occasion at about 9.00 p.m. on a Thursday and again on Friday night at about the same time. Described as being three to four feet tall, six feet in length, with a dark black coat and a long tail, the sightings followed a number of similar reports of a panther-like creature seen prowling about the fields on the outskirts of the town.

Simon Voyle, one of the patrol men, noted: "The first time I saw it, I was walking through the park with a friend, in the pitch dark with my torch after chaining up the gates. It was the length of large filing cabinet and had a curled-up tail. We thought it was our imaginations, but the next night we saw it again. Its eyes were bright yellow."

Voyle was to encounter the beast again: "The second time we were scared because we were stood in the middle of the park by the miniature-golf green, which wasn't a clever place to stand."

Police Constable Adam Brown, of Frome Police Station, was reported to have said that he was concerned that the enigmatic animal may have moved into an urban area, although Frome Town Council appeared much less worried, stating that the public should not be frightened as the unidentified beast was probably more scared of them than they of it.

In July 2010, the *Whitehaven News* website reported that a mystery cat, described as the size of a Labrador dog, had been spotted on Steel Brow at 7.30 a.m., near Arlecdon in West Cumbria.

The witness, who asked to remain nameless, stated: "[It] was very unusual. I have not seen anything like it wild in the British Isles. I was driving to work, from

Arlecdon to Whitehaven, and got to the bottom of the hill, over the bridge, and was about a quarter of the way up. The animal came out of the hedge and onto the road. At first, I thought it was a small roe deer as I have seen these several times on the same journey. I became suspicious as it was too low to the ground to be a deer and had cat-like features."

He also noted that it was light brown in colour, had a long and thick tail, and, after making its way across the road, went through an open gate on the right-hand side before disappearing.

Whereas this sighting was rather benign, the same could not be said about the following, which was reported on 19 December 2008 on the *BBC News* website, in which an elderly woman claimed to be attacked by a large cat in the Highlands.

Pat MacLeod, from Ardross Road in Alness, told police she suffered deep cuts to her legs, as well as cuts and scratches on her hands, and needed stitches after she was attacked by a three-foot-long cat while putting out her rubbish bins. The cat was described as grey in colour, with MacLeod stating that it was the second time she had been attacked by it. She also aired concerns about what may happen if the cat came across a child, given its strength and size.

The local police, who took the attack report seriously, noted that unprovoked attacks were extremely uncharacteristic of a Scottish wildcat and suggested that the animal may have been a hybrid of a domestic and feral cat. Just to be safe, they also suggested that anyone seeing an unusually large cat should not approach it or try to feed it.

In August 2008, a man in Bexley reported that, at around 3.00 a.m. on a Saturday, he was woken up by something screeching and, upon looking out a window, saw a small animal running along a pathway, followed by a larger one. He noted: "I saw a black animal rolling on the grass between two trees. I thought to myself, 'Bloody hell! That's the biggest moggy I've ever seen,' and then thought, 'It must be a dog'. However, its head was cat-like and its tail was very long".

The giant cat then moved off into some bushes, leaving the witness perplexed as to what he had seen. The sighting was reported to the Kent Big Cat Research group, which studies eyewitness reports of large exotic cats, and they believe the creature, which has become known as the Beast of Bexley, was a black leopard and apparently has been seen at Welling, Erith, Bexleyheath, Belvedere, Bromley, Abbey Wood and towards Dartford.

But it's not just enormous cats that appear in suburbia or in wild and rugged areas as, in 2007, near Hound Tor on Dartmoor, a photograph emerged in the press of a strange creature with a thick, shaggy coat, rounded ears, and large front limbs. And, whereas some suggest it is simply a wild dog or a cat, others believe it to be a wolverine or a bear. Whatever the case, the Beast of Dartmoor is real, and local farmers feared that it would prey on their stock.

Martin Whitley, who photographed the creature, stated: "It was walking along a path, about two hundred yards away from me. It was black and grey and comparable in size to a miniature pony. It had very thick shoulders, a long, thick tail with a blunt end, and small round ears. Its movements appeared feline, then bear-like sprang to mind. There was a party climbing the tor opposite, making a racket, but it ignored them completely."

Mr Whitley was also adamant that the creature was not a wild dog, adding: "I have worked with dogs all my life and it was definitely not that. I have seen a collie-sized black cat in the area about ten years ago and it was not that—this was a lot bigger." Notably, he added: "You would be surprised at the number of people who have seen black big cats and something resembling a small bear in the area over the course of the years."

Mark Fraser, the founder of 'Big Cats in Britain' suggested: "It looks like a wolverine or a bear in some shots and a big wild dog in others. It is a very strange animal."

Having said that, the picture does bear some resemblance to an extremely large and hairy boar, and yet speculation as to its true identity still rages. And, as is the case for alien big cats, it is unlikely to go away soon. However, while the identity of this creature is unknown, there is no doubt that it is real—that is, a flesh-and-blood animal and not something from a more paranormal realm, something we shall examine further in the next chapter.

Chapter Five

Vampires and Strange Hairy Men

Highgate Cemetery is located in North London and is an immense sprawling expanse of heavily vegetated land that is divided into two distinct parts: the East and the West. Between the two sections runs a road, Swain's Lane, which separates them. It opened in 1839 as a part of a plan to provide seven large, modern cemeteries around London, as individual church graveyards in London could no longer cope with the number of burials.

Highgate, like the other new cemeteries, became a fashionable place to be buried, with the Victorian attitude to death leading to grand gothic tombs, memorials, mausoleums, catacombs and other architectural structures, including ornate carved angels and Celtic crosses. To get an idea of the scale of the cemetery, there are roughly 167,000 people buried in it, including luminaries such as Karl Marx, Sir Michael Redgrave, Douglas Adams, and Australian artist Sidney Nolan.

In 1983 the cemetery was declared a place of outstanding historic and architectural interest, and a number of funds were set up to ensure that the cemetery would not fall into disrepair, thus ensuring the moss-encrusted tombstones are protected. Since then, English Heritage has assisted in a programme of restoration to the cemetery and although still a working cemetery, it is open to the public for guided tours.

And so it was, on a misty overcast London day in

2010, that I entered the cemetery's grey stone entrance gates for one of these tours.

The cemetery sits on a south-sloping hill and, when opened in the 1800s, would have had outstanding views of the countryside surrounding Highgate Hill. These days, however, the cemetery takes on a dark and almost foreboding nature, due to mature trees, shrubbery and undergrowth, all of which have occurred naturally on the site since maintenance of the grounds was stopped.

Climbing a small set of steps from a paved area outside the entrance gates, the visitor soon finds themselves in an amazing place, resplendent with leaves, moss, fungus, trees, and carved stone structures that valiantly attempt to keep their heads above the encroaching sea of vegetation. It is almost as if one has set foot on the set of a gothic horror movie. The path is gravel, and it crunches where it is dry and squelches noisily when damp, as it winds its way uphill past untold Victorian gravestones and memorials, some as large as small cars. Standing here alone, one could believe that it is haunted; indeed, it has even been reported as having its own resident vampire.

By the 1970s the cemetery had fallen into a dilapidated state of neglect and decay, and stories of ghosts and supernatural occurrences about the place abounded. And it was in this state that stories began to appear about a vampire sighting in the overgrown grounds.

However, previous to this, in 1963 two teenage girls

were walking home along Swain's Lane when they reported seeing what appeared to be mist-like bodies emerging from some graves. Some weeks later, a couple reported seeing a hideous figure hovering behind the iron gates of the cemetery. Soon, other reports started to flood in, including more about the floating figure behind the gate and, with the discovery of some animal carcasses drained of blood, the figure was soon being described as a vampire.

In 1971, a young girl claimed that she was attacked by a vampire in Swain's Lane. She told police that she had been walking along the road when a tall black figure with a deathly white face appeared in front of her before grabbing her and throwing her to the ground. The figure then, apparently, vanished into thin air when a car's headlights appeared. The girl was taken to a nearby police station where she was examined and questioned; the police immediately did a search of the area but could offer no explanation.

Another report emerged after a man went into the cemetery late in the day and, as the light began to fade, he became lost. While looking for a gate to get out, he became aware of something following him and, upon turning, was confronted by a tall dark figure. After a moment of immobility—due to the shock—he fled.

David Farrant, a leading figure in the Highgate Vampire research and who once believed that a vampire could exist within the walls of the cemetery, now tends to discount the vampire theory and instead blames it upon a fascination with horror films and a mild hysteria in reporting. Having said that, the reports of the tall black figure have not stopped, the most recent being in 2005.

Vampire folklore in England, indeed in the whole of the British Isles, is surprisingly common. This is most probably due to the fact that the vampire legend in England is mostly based upon contemporary images of vampires in black capes, with mesmerising eyes, who suck blood from the throats of nubile young women. Given the penchant for Victorian England to be somewhat titillated by such images, we find that vampire lore in England is slightly different from that in Eastern Europe.

Leaving aside the Bram Stoker version of a vampire, which was first published in 1897, we find that the word *vampire* did not even exist in the English language until around 1730. And yet still we find that many old societies have traditions associated with the dead, which are reflected in vampire beliefs.

The return of the dead to feast on the blood of the living is a common occurrence in most cultures. In many of these cases it was thought that the undead person had previously committed a cardinal sin, committed suicide, died on the gallows, or had a black cat jump over their grave—again, all things that are echoed in modern vampire myths.

These people, especially those who had committed suicide or were hanged, were often buried at a crossroads, which was supposed to confuse them when they arose from the grave to start their night-time wanderings.

Often, they were pinned with a stake in their chest, again to stop them from arising. Indeed, so scared were people of the dead arising that protections against vampires were numerous. Iron was thought able to repel them, and garlic was also used, most probably because of its medicinal properties and its reputation for being something of a repellent to other inhabitants of the underworld. In fact, garlic was so popular that it is widely seen today in movies and television programmes as something that unfailingly wards off vampires.

Of course, vampire myths are just that: myths. However, the drinking of blood (an important part of vampire lore) has been for hundreds, maybe thousands, of years an important part of some societies, as it was believed that the blood held the life force of a creature. As such, drinking the blood of that creature was to absorb its life force, its energy, and its power. This has obvious parallels with vampire lore, given that a vampire drinks living blood so as to gain life, even though this life is, paradoxically, as one of the undead.

Some early medieval chroniclers recorded a number of folk tales that have vampiric overtones. William of Newburgh, a twelfth-century writer and a monk, once described an occasion where a recently dead man returned from the grave in the form of a spectre and was seen by his widow and other relatives. To drive him away, the family stayed up at night and made lots of noise. Sadly, William recounted, this made matters worse as the man soon began to appear in daylight and required the intervention of the Bishop of Lincoln, who advised that the body be exhumed and burned. When the body was exhumed, it was reported that it was still as fresh as the day it had been buried. The family then duly cremated the body, and the spectre was seen no more.

And even further back in the mists of time, we find a report from around the year 1138 about 'the Hunderprest', meaning 'dog-priest', the nickname given to a priest at Melrose Abbey in the Scottish Borders. He was given the nickname because his favourite pastime was hunting on horseback with a pack of dogs. The Hunderprest had a reputation for being a somewhat evil character, so when he died he returned as a revenant and he was forced to drink the blood of innocents and change into a bat. Legend has it that the monks were content to let him wander around, undead—until he began to bother his mistress for sex.

Eventually, the monks and priests banded together in order to bring an end to his nefarious nocturnal wanderings. They waited at the Hunderprest's grave until he arose at nightfall when they attacked him, knocking him down with the blow of an axe to his head. They quickly cremated the vampire's body and spread his ashes, which apparently ended his reign of terror. However, some say that his ghost still haunts the area.

Also in Scotland, this time at Gorbals graveyard in Glasgow, a vampire with iron teeth apparently kidnapped two children. However, within a few hours, the graveyard was full of children with makeshift weapons, such as sticks and knives, hunting for the vampire. At the time, authorities blamed the occurrence on hysteria and the influence of American comics like *Tales From The*

Crypt, but it has since been noted out that there were no comics from this period featuring vampires with iron teeth. Is it possible that there was some truth to the iron-toothed vampire? And if so, did dozens of armed children, all intent on killing the creature, scared it away, never to return?

But such reports may not be as unusual as we think: over the past hundred years, Britain has recorded over two hundred stories about vampires. Indeed, paranormal investigator, the Reverend Lionel Fanthorpe notes that there are around two alleged sightings per year: "I really only expected to find one or two instances in Britain, so I was amazed when I discovered one story after another. And I really didn't expect to find more here than in somewhere like Transylvania. It is in a part of Europe where folklore and fairy tales are widespread, but in fact we could find only nine or ten reports there, over the same period."

Fanthorpe believes that there are numerous explanations as to why there are so many sightings in Britain, including the publication of Bram Stoker's *Dracula*, which was set in the seaside town of Whitby in North Yorkshire, and the fact that Britain has historically been invaded numerous times. He explained: "We are an island nation, where many people have come in from other parts of the world—Romans, Anglo-Saxons, Vikings. So, if these creatures came here as part of invasions, they stayed and had no means of getting out again."

Indeed, if Fanthorpe is correct, then the United

Kingdom is a veritable hotspot for vampire sightings. For example, a woman from Surrey claimed that on three separate occasions over three months in 1938 she was attacked by some sort of vampire. While many people believed it was an animal that may have escaped from a zoo, the mystery was never solved.

It is said that in the late eighteenth century William Doggett stole thousands of pounds from his master after the master had moved abroad from Eastbury House, near Blandford in Dorset. When his master returned, Doggett shot himself. However, not long afterwards he was seen lurking around the village at night, his blood-covered face testament to his violent demise. When his body was exhumed in 1845 it had not decomposed and had a rosy tint to the cheeks.

Alnwick Castle in Northumberland was built after the Norman Conquest of 1066. Over the years it has been renovated and remodelled a number of times. It is currently the home of the Duke of Northumberland and hosts hundreds of thousands of visitors each year. However, it was also known as the home of a terrifying vampire who possessed a hunchback and stalked the grounds of the castle at night, spreading death and disease during the Middle Ages. In this case, the local peasants banded together and burned its body, reducing it to ash.

But not all reports are ancient, as evident from the following stories and, although they do not follow the stereotypical report of a vampire, they do possess similar characteristics.

In November of 1899 or 1900, Geoffrey Anderson was walking home when he found himself at the corner of Princes Street and Hanover Street in Edinburgh. Standing there, he noticed a horse and carriage outside a shop, illuminated by the shop's lighting. Suddenly, he saw a black mass that seemed to come out of the drain about fifteen feet away from the horse and carriage. He described the mass changing into a shape similar to that of an hourglass and about four feet long and two feet wide. Although the shape moved, it had no visible legs and was described as moving like a caterpillar. It then sprung at the horse's throat and clung on. Horrified, Anderson and another passer-by ran forward to help the terrified animal. As they did so, the black mass simply vanished into thin air and the horse was unharmed.

In the 1920s, at Glen Tilt, Blair Atholl, in Scotland, two poachers who had retired for the night to rest in a 'bothy' (a shelter, usually an old cottage found in isolated areas) reported that they were suddenly attacked while they slept by some kind of creature that succeeded in drinking some blood from one of the men. After a frightening struggle with the creature, it is said to have flown away or simply vanished.

The next report, also from Edinburgh, is also fascinating in that it too has vampiric elements as well as being treated as a serious murder case, as yet unsolved, of medical student Andrew Muir, who was reported to have been investigating severe paranormal activity at the time of his death.

The supernatural activity appeared to be centred on an

apparition that was witnessed by staff and visitors to William Brien House in Inverleith in the winter of 1915–1916. A number of staff members had quit their jobs and left, and many guests had fled from the hotel in fear, with all claiming to have seen a strange and evil apparition watching them. As a dare, Andrew Muir asked the owners if he could hold an all-night vigil in the most active room to see if he could work out whatever was happening.

The owners agreed but specified that Muir had a bell to ring if he needed to alert them to anything untoward happening. A few hours after the vigil began the owners heard the bell and a scream and rushed back to the room, where they found Muir slumped over, with puncture wounds in his neck and shoulder that were still bleeding.

The murder is still unresolved to this day, although some claim that the apparition was the previous owner of the house, William Brien, who was apparently a very strange person who lived as a recluse. When he died, he left strict instructions that his grave was to be forty feet deep and the coffin to be kept secure at all costs. Whether this was to keep him in or keep something else out is not known, but even now, with the house being converted into a hotel, guests report hearing strange noises, voices and other activity.

Ron Halliday, in his book *Edinburgh After Dark: Vampires, Ghosts and Witches of the Old Town*, notes that a cleaner at the house once "felt an invisible presence standing next to her, so intense and evil that she believed it was trying to take control of her mind. She felt, she said, 'almost hypnotised'. Vampires, it should be noted, have the power of invisibility and try to 'take over' a person before attacking them."

Halliday also notes another strange happening that occurred in the 1970s: A man named Tom Adler was passing a cemetery near Slateford Road and he glimpsed a movement in the shadows: "Frankly, it looked as if the figure was wearing some kind of cloak. A car went by and it seemed to startle 'him'. I assumed it was a *he* but he didn't seem to notice me. It was about 1.00 a.m. so there wasn't anyone else around, and at that point I was more curious than anything. But then something totally weird happened. I know it sounds hard to believe—I can hardly believe it myself—but 'something' seemed to rise out of the ground beside the shadowy figure. My body felt like it had turned to ice in an instant. A voice in my head kept saying, 'It's just a trick. It's just a trick,' but I was petrified. There was just something so weird about it. I must have said something in the middle of all of this, or done something, and the shadowy figure turned and looked straight at me, stepping forward a bit more into the light. It had a human shape but spindly arms and legs. I was utterly panicking and wanted to get away, but I couldn't get anything to move. Next, I saw that the figure that had risen from the ground was facing me. It looked like a woman's shape as it had a kind of flowing garment on. All this happened in seconds, but it felt like a lifetime. I might have stood there forever if the woman hadn't suddenly lifted a couple of feet off the ground and seemed to hover in the air with her arms pointed towards me, like a scene from a horror film. I admit I screamed. I've never been so terrified in my whole life, not even while in the army. But that seemed to break the spell, and I turned and ran."

Vampire or not, I guess we shall never know, although similar occurrences have been reported across Edinburgh and Scotland in general. Was it a trick of light? Maybe steam escaping from a vent? Perhaps a fleeting piece of mist or fog? Or perhaps, just perhaps, Adler witnessed something even more fanciful than we can imagine: a body rising from the grave—in simple terms, the undead.

Elsewhere in Scotland, other reports of vampire-like activity have been recorded: for instance, Glamis Castle, the home of the Earl and Countess of Strathmore and Kinghorne, has a number of bizarre legends attached to it, including two that pertain to vampires.

Glamis Castle has been the ancestral home of the Lyon family since the fourteenth century although the present building dates largely from the seventeenth century. It was the childhood home of the Queen Mother, wife of King George VI; their second daughter, Princess Margaret, Countess of Snowdon, was born there. But before we get to the vampire legends of the castle, we should first look at the most famous legend attached to this picturesque, ancient building.

The most famous story connected with the castle is that of the Monster of Glamis, who was apparently a hideously deformed child who was kept in the castle all his life and his suite of rooms bricked up after his death. Some accounts of the monster were recorded by singer and composer Virginia Gabriel, who stayed at the castle in 1870. Interestingly, a tale attached to this tells of guests who were staying at Glamis and, in an attempt to find the monster's rooms, hung towels from the windows of every room. When they examined the castle from the outside, they found several windows were towel-free.

Of course, Glamis Castle has numerous legends about ghostly figures that waft their way through its stately rooms and corridors. These include a Grey Lady who is said to haunt the castle chapel and is thought to be the spirit of Janet Douglas, Lady Glamis, who was burned at the stake outside Edinburgh Castle in 1537; a 'tongueless' woman who is said to roam the castle grounds late at night, an eerie face that appears at one of the upper windows; and a tall, thin figure in a long black cloak who terrorises guests. As well, the spirit of Earl Beardie is said to stalk the halls of the castle late at night. Several guests have reported waking in the small hours to find the Earl's lifeless face looming over them.

Glamis Castle is, unsurprisingly, believed to be one of the most haunted buildings in Britain, with strange and mysterious phenomena, unexplained happenings and manifestations being regularly experienced within the castle walls. Indeed, Shakespeare used Glamis as the setting for *Macbeth*. Sir Walter Scott, on staying there alone for a night noted that, while there he felt "as too far from the living and somewhat too near to the dead".

However, if the monster of Glamis was no more than a deformed child, and we are not really all that interested in ghosts, then what of the castle's other folk tales, those of vampiric creatures?

The first vampiric tale from the castle concerns that of a child who was born to the family and who was suspected of being a vampire. The child was later locked away in a separate, secure room for its own safety as well as for the safety of the residents of the castle. Further legend also suggests that within each generation of the family, one of them will be a vampire.

But whereas this is simply old folk tales, the next, about a bloodsucking woman is not so easily dismissed as, a few hundred years ago, a serving woman employed at the castle was caught leaning over a body and drinking the victim's blood. She was immediately proclaimed a vampire and was walled up alive in a secret room in the castle. Some believe that even today the vampire is still alive and waiting to be released.

But it's not just England and Scotland where these bizarre encounters have been reported. Derelict Baron Hill Hall in Anglesey, Wales, also has a bloody history of vampirism. Legend has it that the ghost of a young girl, the youngest member of the ancestral Bulkeley family, still roams the grounds at night, and it is suspected that she is a vampire because, while the rest of the house lies in ruins, the tomb in which her body was interred remains intact, locked and bolted.

The vampire of Berwick is another similar vampire story. In this case, the vampire was the ghost of a man who, while alive, was extremely wealthy, but also sinful and nasty to all. It is believed he died of the plague, which was ever-present in England in the Middle Ages. Being a nasty and sinful man, he was hurriedly buried in unconsecrated land. However, to the consternation of villagers, he was soon spotted roaming the town as a pale phantom, accompanied by a pack of black hounds. Where he went, plague followed—and the townsfolk became so worried that they dug up his body, cut it into small pieces and then burned them. Apparently, this did the trick: the man was never seen again, and the plague reportedly cleared up—at least, until the next infection broke out, which, sadly, in the Middle Ages, would not have been very long.

Further British folklore also hints at other vampiric creatures. In the Highlands of Scotland some remote valleys are said to be haunted by dangerous and evil female spirits called *Boabhan Sith* or the White Woman of the Highlands. These spirits are said to be beautiful seductresses in green dresses who prey on young travellers by night and who, once a year, arise from their graves to feed on young men by night, in forests or other natural places away from towns and cities and other inhabited areas. Operating in groups, they are said to seduce their victims and, after dancing with them, drink their blood, using sharp fingernails rather than fangs to draw the life-giving fluid.

The history of vampires appears to show that they can physically change their bodies at will—that is, transform into a rat or a wolf or some other creature. And yet it also appears that they can exist as shadowy or ghost-like entities, not quite fully formed and something similar to an incubus or succubus, the creatures of medieval folklore that appear at night and attempt to have sexual intercourse with sleeping persons. But, as these creatures are not quite fully flesh and blood, do they exist in another, parallel world and visit ours from time to time to feast on what is essentially our life force? Or are they all around us all the time, simply waiting for the chance to attack? Sandra Donald, a woman in her forties who had just experienced a messy divorce, believes this to be so.

She noted: "After we split, I bought a small flat in Leith. This was around August 1981. I was pleased to have a place of my own and felt I had a start in rebuilding my life again. I really liked my new home and it was very handy for getting to town, where I worked. I was in a bit of turmoil because of everything I'd been through, but there's no way that explained what happened. One day the atmosphere in the flat just seemed to change. I'd felt fine there, but after I came home from work one evening—I think it was October—the atmosphere seemed all heavy and depressed. I couldn't put my finger on it and thought it was just my imagination. But that night in bed I had a strange dream that something human-like, not fully like a man, put his mouth over mine, but wasn't kissing me, more sucking the air from my mouth. I woke up in fright and thought I saw something, I'm not sure what, disappear out the window. I was terrified and stayed awake for ages. I thought, 'You've been working too hard. It's just a daft dream'. The following night nothing happened but the night after I had that horrible dream again. I woke, and swear I saw what looked like that man-thing again, disappearing out the window, but I got a better sight of it. It looked like a man's shape, but I could see through his body. I really felt alone and vulnerable and went into the sitting room where I dozed in the chair till morning. The next night I forced myself to go to bed, left the bedside lamp on and slept right through. And I never had that dream again, though the atmosphere in the flat was still oppressive. Now I realised I was getting listless. I thought at first it was because I'd lost sleep, but I was getting a good sleep and still feeling washed out. People began to tell me I looked tired and pale. And it was true. My energy seemed to be going down to nothing. I became convinced that it was the flat. I hated to admit it because I'd been so proud of it and loved the place. I moved in with my mum, though I didn't tell her why, just saying I needed some company. Two weeks later I went back to the flat and the whole feeling of the place was better. It made me feel better too. I was a bit nervous when I started sleeping there again, but nothing happened. The place seemed like it was back to normal. I have no idea what happened to me, but it was a horrible experience. I felt that I'd been used by something. God knows what, and I'd rather not find out, to be honest."

Although Donald did not suffer physical harm, it appears that she was subjected to an attack by a psychic vampire, which in mythology sucks the life force out of a person, as opposed to their blood. However, as our next story will show, vampire lore in the British Isles is generally contained to the bloodsucking, undead phantom of the night, more akin to Bram Stoker's Dracula than some ethereal apparition.

The phantom of Croglin Grange is one of the best-known vampire stories in Britain. It is almost as famous in vampire lore as *Dracula*, although the story, which appeared in a book called *In My Solitary Life* by

Augustus Hare, was probably fabricated at the time to impress guests or friends.

Croglin itself is a quiet, picturesque village near the Pennines and the River Eden. The surrounding land is used for agriculture, mainly sheep, and a small river, Croglin Water, flows through the valley down into the River Eden. A village has existed in this location for a long time and may originally have been two separate hamlets. There has been a church on the current site since the Norman period, although the present building was built in 1878. Apart from these things of interest, there is a post office and a pub—and a vampire legend.

The vampire legend of Croglin Grange is interesting, in that it is one of the more fully documented cases in vampire lore anywhere in the world. Sadly, there is some doubt about its veracity, but, even then, it makes for interesting reading.

In the early nineteenth century, the Fisher family moved from Croglin Grange to larger dwellings and put the property up for let. The Grange itself sat uninhabited for quite a long period of time before it was finally rented by the Cranwells, consisting of two brothers and a sister, Michael, Edward and Amelia. The Cranwells seemed happy with life and soon settled, socialising with the locals and become well respected in the area.

One balmy summer night, Amelia Cranwell lay on her bed with the bedclothes cast off because of the heat. The windows were closed, but the shutters were not fastened. As Amelia gazed out of the window into the fading light, she became aware of two lights that looked like eyes moving around in a nearby graveyard. Feeling uneasy, and slightly frightened, she shut the window tight, bolted the door and then lay down in her bed to try and get some sleep.

Close to sleep, she was suddenly jolted awake by a scratching sound from outside the window. Sitting up, she looked at the window and saw the two eyes that she had previously seen in the graveyard. This time, however, they were burning like coals, and she realised that she was looking at some sort of demonic creature. She tried to scream, but no sound came from her terrified mouth.

Frozen in fear, she watched as the creature slowly started picking at the triangular glass frames in the window, until enough had fallen out for it to reach in and unlock the latch. The creature then smoothly climbed into the room, where the defenceless Amelia remained transfixed and terrified on the bed. Towering above her with burning eyes and blood-red lips, the frightening figure stooped down and pulled her head back. The brothers, Edward and Michael, who were sleeping in an adjacent room, were awoken by the commotion and, fearing something tragic had befallen their sister, they tried to open her door.

Unfortunately, the door was locked and the brothers were forced to smash it open with a poker. Inside the room there was a stench of mould and decay, and on the bed lay their sister Amelia, blood pumping from arterial gashes in her neck. One of the brothers rushed to the open window and just caught sight of the shadow of a tall man-like figure scurrying across the bottom of the lawn, near the churchyard. The brothers immediately tended their sister's wounds, and managed to revive her, saving her from bleeding to death.

With Amelia surviving this horrific attack, the Cranwells decided to move to Switzerland so as to allow the girl to recuperate in the clear mountain air. While in Switzerland the brothers swore revenge on the creature. Surprisingly, when Amelia heard of this revenge, she offered herself as bait and would not be dissuaded by her brothers, who rightly feared for her safety.

And so, the Cranwells returned to Croglin and prepared to meet whatever it was that had invaded their house many months ago. Amelia took her place in the bedroom where she had been previously attacked and, as the moon rose, sure enough a pair of glaring eyes became evident in the graveyard. The eyes moved closer to the house, and soon grey, dead-like hands were picking at the pieces of window glass.

The creature then, as before, removed enough glass so as to be able to open the window and then leapt into the room. However, this time Edward and Michael were waiting, having hidden themselves. Both men fired at the creature with pistols and it leapt out of the window, emitting a low howl. Then they rushed to the open window and watched as it fled across the lawn towards the graveyard. Frightened, and not wanting to follow the creature at night, the family waited for morning.

In the morning Amelia was moved to safety, and the

townsfolk gathered to search for the creature. There appeared to be no signs of disturbance in the graveyard, so they turned their attention to the church, where they noticed that a crypt door was slightly ajar. Apprehensively, the two brothers pushed open the door and were greeted by a gruesome sight—for there, inside the crypt, lay broken coffins and human bones, which appeared to have teeth marks upon them.

In all the chaos, however, they noticed that one coffin appeared to be untouched. The villagers tore off its lid and there inside, wrapped in evil-smelling and mouldy clothes, was the creature, its eyes cold and dead, its hands grey and lifeless. And yet, on one of its legs was a fresh pistol wound.

Not surprisingly, given the circumstances, the villagers are said to have dragged the coffin and its contents out into the churchyard, constructed a large fire, and burned the lot, presumably killing whatever the human-like creature was. No one in the village seemed to know why or where the creature came from, or why it had lain dormant for so long. Whatever the case, it was never seen or heard of again.

In the early 1920s Charles Harper, a London-born author and illustrator, visited the area and challenged the veracity of the story. Although he found two similar buildings, Croglin High Hall and Croglin Low Hall, he could find no place called Croglin Grange. In addition, there were no vaults or crypts as described in the original story.

Interestingly, Harper's own account was later challenged when Francis Clive-Ross, also a publisher and author and whose works focused on occultism and comparative religion, later visited the area. Clive-Ross determined that the Croglin Low Hall was indeed the house mentioned in the story and that a chapel had existed in close proximity to the house many years previous to Harper's visit.

Modern-day researchers have pointed out the similarities between the Croglin Grove vampire and *Varney the Vampyre, the Feast of Blood,* a serialised mid-Victorian gothic horror story by James Rymer, which would suggest that the story is simply fiction, a parlour story thought up by Augustus Hare to entertain guests, as both Hare's book, *In My Solitary Life*, and *Varney* were published in the late 1920s.

Strangely, though, Clive-Ross later discussed the story with residents of the village and was told that Hare had made a significant mistake in his retelling of the story—that is, Hare's story was set in the 1870s, whereas the original story was from the late 1600s. This would place the story well before *Varney the Vampyre* and even well before most vampire legends in England.

But not all vampires seem to crave human blood, as in 1991, after hearing stories from locals of animals being found drained of blood, Tom Robertson, a self-styled ghost hunter, and his wife visited Lochmaben Castle near Lockerbie, searching for evidence of the supernatural and ghosts. Leaving his wife in the car, he walked into the woods, where he found numerous bodies of small animals. Puzzled, he continued on until he became aware of a tall figure "dressed in sacking, with a hood over its head". The creature leapt into a tree and swung away. Realising he had left his wife alone, he ran back to the car, and together they rapidly drove away, Robertson later commenting that "[t]here is a creature slinking around in those woods, baying for blood".

But if vampires are more the stuff of legend and myth and fall into a supernatural category, then what of our next strange creatures? Those being frightening, hairy men, somewhat similar to the American Bigfoot or the Australian Yowie.

In November 2005 the *Huffington Post* ran an article proclaiming that a British dog walker had photographed what appeared to be a Yeti in Sussex. The creature, quickly dubbed the 'British Bigfoot' by the press was first spotted by Caroline Toms' dog, Ash, who was frightened by the ape-like creature while walking in woods.

Toms recalled: "It all happened so fast. Ash started acting a little bit bemused and barking. Then she, quick as a flash, shot off into the undergrowth—then I saw this big black thing flash out in front of me. I only had my camera out because I was taking pictures of Ash playing. She came running back, quick as a flash, though. I don't know what it was, but when I had a closer look at the pictures, it certainly does look like Bigfoot to me."

Toms added: "I think it could be Bigfoot, but it happened so fast I cannot be absolutely certain. It was just luck I had the camera out. It was so big and massive,

I don't know if it could be anything else."

However, a spokesperson from the British Big Cat Society, when asked if the image could be a wild cat, was rather dismissive: "That is a bloke in a suit. One hundred percent."

But if such a report seems strange for the English countryside, then think again, as reports of 'hairy' men' are really not that uncommon.

Kent is known as the garden of England. It is a large patchwork quilt of rolling hills of various shades of greens and yellows, with small roads that snake along ancient field boundaries from historic town to historic town. Crystal-clear rivers and streams burble merrily as they wind their way through this green and leafy wonderland, and historic castles and buildings dot the landscape as thick as bees around a honey pot.

And yet it is not these castles that interest us, as Kent has, bizarrely, been subject to sporadic sightings of strange, wild, hairy men.

In May of 1961 at Bilsington, two schoolgirls reportedly watched in horror as a hairy man-beast with a tail walked out of a forested area into a field, where it stood for some time before turning and running back into the trees. Then in 1997 an anonymous person wrote to the Kent Messenger Group, explaining how he'd seen a large gorilla-like creature in some woods not far from Maidstone.

Dubbed the 'Kentish Apeman', the creature is said to be eight feet tall and covered in hair, with red, demonic eyes. The most recent sighting is believed to have taken place last month on Tunbridge Wells Common, a two-hundred-acre wooded site which sits in the centre of the town and is one of its most picturesque features.

A local resident, Graham S., recalled on a website how he was working as a painter in the house of an elderly lady when she told him of an experience in which she came face to face with the apeman on the Common during World War II. The post read: "One particular day she went to the Common with her husband and was sitting on a bench when they became aware of a shuffling noise behind them. Upon turning around, both her husband and herself saw what she described as a tall, hairy, ape-like creature with eyes that were burning a reddish colour, and it was moving towards them at a slow pace. They observed this creature for some time until they became afraid and they both fled—terrified. She went on to say that they told the police and members of their family, thinking that a gorilla had escaped from a zoo, but were laughed at and were not believed."

Another sighting, by a girl known only as Charlotte, took place in Dartford when she was driving home from the University of Kent. She said she saw a creature with long arms, and knees that came up under its chin as it walked. She was so frightened she nearly crashed her car.

Other sightings include five members of the Territorial Army in 1991, spotting the beast on Blue Bell Hill, near Maidstone, and throwing stones and shouting at it before running away. In Chatham, a young girl and her partner saw the apeman appear then run off into the bushes.

But these odd sightings, few as they may be, seem to occur all over southeast England. At Winterfold in Surrey in 1967 a motorist pulled over to clean his windscreen when he noticed a huge figure standing further down the road. Strangely, this beast seemed to have a glowing head. However, even more surprising is that it was reported to have a foul odour, something that is often reported by people who claim to have seen, or been in close proximity to, a Bigfoot or Yowie.

And then some forty-five years later, on the night of 18 November 2002, at Friston Park in neighbouring Sussex, a lorry driver parked his vehicle by the side of the road to have a rest and stretch his legs when he noticed a large, hairy creature in the trees. Unsettled by this sighting, he shone a torch at the creature, which disappeared into the darkness.

Following this, another report in February 2006 described a strange low-pitched noise coming from dark woods at the end of a garden. As the witness walked cautiously towards the woods, he noticed what appeared to be two eyes. Not surprisingly, the person panicked and switched on some security lights, which revealed what he believed to be two eyes on a strange, hairy head. He then fled back to his house.

Having said that, perhaps nothing compares with the recent reports of Cannock Chase, a large forested area in central England that has become a veritable mecca for those seeking the paranormal or supernatural, with reported encounters of big cats, black dogs, Bigfoot-like creatures, and, incredibly, werewolves.

In April 2007, the local newspaper stated that there had been a glut of werewolf sightings on the outskirts of the West Midlands town of Stafford. A local paranormal group was quick to investigate and were shocked to be contacted by numerous residents who claimed that they had seen a hairy wolf-like creature walking on its hind legs, like a man. When spotted, it apparently ran away into the nearby woods.

The local postman told the paranormal group that he had seen what he thought was a large dog wandering around a nearby cemetery. When he walked over to investigate, he was horrified to see the creature rise up onto its hind legs and run away. Earlier, another report, this time from a scoutmaster, suggested that the creature, when on its hind legs, was six to seven feet tall—which leads us to consider, is this a werewolf we are talking about, or something else, perhaps something similar to the American Bigfoot?

Indeed, the *Birmingham Post* reported: "A tribe of subterranean creatures who surface on Cannock Chase to hunt for food could be behind a rash of werewolf and Bigfoot sightings near Stafford," and that "[t]he mysterious beings could also be responsible for a string of pet disappearances."

Another paranormal expert put forward the theory that the subhuman beast was not a werewolf or Bigfoot at all, but a Stone Age throwback—in simple terms, a Neanderthal. The person, who for obvious reasons wished to remain anonymous, stated: "Strange sightings in this area have been made over many years by civilians, military, police, ex-police and scout leaders on patrol."

But it's not just Cannock Chase where strange reports of werewolf-like creatures appear. As recently as May 2016, a number of werewolf sightings were reported in woods outside of Hull, sparking local residents to organise a hunt for the beast on the next full moon. According to witnesses who came forward, over the past few months a huge, hairy creature had been spotted around the Barmston Drain, a man-made channel near the town of Beverley, with some locals believing that the creature to be that of the mythical Yorkshire beast called 'Old Stinker'.

'Old Stinker' is said to haunt the Yorkshire Wolds, an area of stunningly picturesque countryside north of the Barmston Drain. More specifically, however, the creature is supposed to stalk the Wold Newton Triangle, an area widely known for mysterious activity, including stories of ghosts, zombies, vampires, and other paranormal occurrences, including 'Old Stinker', so called because of its terrible bad breath.

Charles Christian, a local author and expert on the subject, speaking to the *Hull Daily Mail*, stated: "The Yorkshire Wolds was actually one of the last parts of England to have wild wolves. Old Stinker was said to be operating on the other side of them, but it would be no distance at all for a large animal to get to Hull. When you get multiple sightings, combined with a tradition of stories going back centuries, it is hard to ignore the possibility something might be there."

He also noted, ominously, that when in the area, "people would glimpse what they thought was the rear lights of a car in front, [and] it would instead reveal itself to be the red eyes of a wolf".

One woman, who wished to remain nameless when speaking to the *Express*, told how she had seen the creature in December of the previous year, noting that it ran both on two legs or, alternatively, on all fours, as if it was part human and part wolf. She stated that it "was [standing] upright one moment … the next, it was down on all fours, running like a dog. [She] was terrified. It vaulted thirty feet over to the other side, and vanished up the embankment and over a wall into some allotments."

Another couple said they saw something they described as "tall and hairy" eating a dog, next to the channel which runs through the countryside. They noted, to their amazement, that it leapt effortlessly over an eight-foot fence, with the dog in its mouth.

And in another report, a woman who was walking her dog spotted something "half dog, half human", and she noted that her dog refused to go any further along the path they were walking along.

But if 'Old Stinker' haunts the Yorkshire Wolds and Hull, then what of reports of a werewolf in London, to quote singer-songwriter Warren Zevon?

In October 1996 there was a curious report of a frightening and inexplicable encounter with what can be only described as a werewolf-like creature in Camberwell Old Cemetery.

Camberwell Old Cemetery is located on Forest Hill Road and covers approximately thirty acres. Like the infamous Highgate Cemetery, it was established in the mid-nineteenth century to solve the problem of overcrowding in churchyards, with the first burial taking place in 1856. As of the 1980s, over 300,000 burials have taken place, so one would suspect that the place would be more awash with ghost stories rather than those of werewolves.

However, on this occasion, a man was on his way to meet a friend when he had to pass the cemetery one night. Deciding to cut through the cemetery to save twenty minutes' walking, he found himself in the middle of the graveyard when something caught his eye. Looking around in the darkness, he saw something large and dark which, he thought, was "a dog, a big dog, move very quickly".

Stopping for a moment, he squinted into the darkness before moving off, when: "I thought that somebody had literally run into me and knocked me over... Something had grabbed me by my arm, very tightly, and smashed me to the ground. It was big, it was powerful, and it had extremely bad breath and it smelled cold and awful. This thing was now bearing down on me, looking directly at my face, dribbling onto me and growling."

The creature then sniffed him up and down, much like a dog would do, and the man stated later that "[he] was convinced [he] was going to die."

Then to his surprise and relief, it sprinted away on its hind legs.

The man later stated: "Part of me wants to be rational and say it was a strong man in a costume, but that's my mind wanting to say, *stop being stupid*. But if that's the case, it was the best costume I've ever seen, [and must have been] worn by an Olympic athlete due to the speed and strength."

What could the creature have been? Possibly a very large dog or a person in an ape suit? Maybe it was nothing more than a guard dog, given that it breathed a nauseating breath on him and sniffed his body like a dog would do. And yet, if a guard dog, then it would have barked and not moved away. As for its size, true, there are dogs that can grow to immense sizes and weights, but they cannot run on their hind legs. Is it possible that the man met an infamous 'black dog' while taking a shortcut through the cemetery, given that black dog sightings often happen in such places? Or, even more fanciful, had he encountered what we consider to be a werewolf—that is, a human able to change its physical form into that of a wolf, while retaining a few human characteristics of a human? Whatever the case, the man has not ventured into the cemetery since.

Interestingly, in January 1879, a man was taking a cart of luggage from Ranton in Staffordshire to Woodcock in Shropshire. He was late in coming back, and his horse was tired so could only walk at a gentle pace. At about ten o'clock he arrived where the road crossed the Liverpool and Birmingham Canal. Just before he reached the canal bridge, a strange black creature with huge white eyes leapt from the roadside bushes onto the back of the horse. The man hit at the creature with his whip but was horrified when the whip went through the creature as if it didn't exist.

The horse, previously so exhausted that it could barely walk, suddenly found a new lease of life, broke into a gallop and sped off down the dark road with the creature apparently clinging to its back. The terrified man quickly found lodgings and told his tale to all who would listen, apparently scaring one of the pub's patrons so much that he refused to go home that night, preferring to stay the night rather than cross the seemingly haunted bridge.

The man who had witnessed this strange apparition reportedly took some days to come back to his senses, and when he did, he was visited by a policeman who came to request some information from him about the event, assuming that it had been a failed robbery. The man, now recovered from his strange ordeal, stated that he was not robbed and then related the story to the policeman. He was then left incredulous when the policeman informed him that what he'd encountered was the 'man-monkey' who had been appearing at the bridge at night ever since a man drowned in the canal.

Although strange and quite unbelievable, what are we to make of this encounter? Did the lonely traveller and his horse really come across the spirit of a man who once drowned in the canal? If so, it would be a simple ghost story and explanations would be relatively easy to put forward. And yet, this ghost was hairy, a 'monkey-man', and therefore seemingly similar to other large, hairy men that have been reported throughout history, such as Bigfoot, Yetis, and Yowies. And yet, this was apparently a ghost, the size of a man, which leads us to ask, if the encounter were true, is this a hairy ghost, or are large, hairy men—somehow not of this world—existing in some strange sort of unknown supernatural realm?

And, if this is so, then do the American Bigfoot, Australian Yowie and Himalayan Yeti exist as a solid flesh-and-blood being, or as something much more mysterious and disturbing: creatures that transcend space and time? Or have we got the whole story wrong? Could this hairy man-beast be the feared werewolf of medieval folklore? And if so, why is this werewolf a ghost rather than a being of flesh and blood like the werewolves of legend?

Whatever the case, the reports keep emerging. For instance, at around 7.15 p.m. on 24 January 2015, David Youell claimed that he came across a half-man, half-ape type beast in Hopwas Woods, Tamworth, in Staffordshire, whilst out walking his dogs.

Youell said he was alerted to the creature when both his dogs started barking loudly: "It was crouching down—I thought it was a bear for a moment. Then it sprang up on two legs and it was enormous, about seven feet tall with long, shaggy hair or fur. I didn't see its face, it just bounded across the path and into the woods and I could hear it crashing through the undergrowth. For the life of me, I'm not sure what it was, but it was big and had dark, shaggy hair. It was upright, but its back was bent over. Whatever it was, it certainly made me jump."

Then, in January 2015, the *Courier* revealed that a Fife man had broken ten years of silence about an encounter he had with a Bigfoot-like creature just off the Tay Road Bridge in 2005.

The man, who wished to remain anonymous, said the encounter happened in August 2005 at around 3.40 a.m. at the Five Roads roundabout on the A92 when he was driving home from work: "After navigating the Five Roads roundabout, I was proceeding home on the A92 when my headlights picked out what I thought was a man standing by the left-hand side of the road. As I approached, the figure stepped out in front of my car and I naturally brought it to a halt to avoid hitting the individual. This 'person' was a large, hairy ape-like creature, which turned to look at the car as I approached. Its eyes gave out a shine that was very noticeable and it crossed the road in about three large strides."

Puzzled by the encounter, the man stopped the car and wound down the window, noting: "I could hear something like crunching, as something was clearly moving through the forest, but I had no torch with me to shine towards the sounds. There was an unpleasant odour in the air, and suddenly I got a feeling I was being watched as everything went very quiet. I then continued home. Thinking back, this individual was well over seven feet tall and a dark brown colour. Its hair was of reasonable length. I have never seen this again anywhere in Scotland and only confided in my partner."

And he added: "I know unequivocally what I saw, and it is still clear in my mind as if it happened yesterday."

Around the same time, Charmaine Fraser from Edinburgh revealed how she had also seen a seven-foot-tall black beast with no neck and broad shoulders, near a disused sandstone quarry during a morning walk with her grandmother's dog, as a child in Carmyllie in Scotland in the early 1980s.

She told *The Courier* in 2015: "I was with the dog and we were coming down the path that leads to the track running past the bottom of the property and out to the farm road. Just before I got on to the track, the dog stopped suddenly and started to growl, whine, and bare her teeth. I looked up to see a large black figure further along the track, standing with its back to me. It was reaching up to a branch on a tree at the side of the track and was tall, of thick build, with no neck and wide shoulders. I remember standing in shock for a second or two before screaming and turning to run back to the house. As I screamed, it slowly started to turn round, but I didn't hang about to see its face."

Fraser, who has a degree in psychology from St Andrews University, also said that she had seen the same creature not long after her first sighting, and it was "like a gorilla standing upright," and a "humanoid shape" with "eyes that shone orange when headlights picked it out in the darkness".

In late 2015, Adam Bird claimed to have taken a photograph of a Bigfoot-like creature looming ominously behind a tree in a Lincolnshire wood. Bird, co-founder of British Bigfoot Research, captured the picture while out walking in the Friskney nature reserve

After hearing of previous Bigfoot sightings in the area, Bird decided to go and have a look himself and so ventured into the woods with a camera, to search for clues as to the identity of the mysterious beast. He claimed to have followed some strange noises and large human-like footprints before capturing the image: "My investigators and I were tipped off that this small patch of woodland in Friskney could be a hotspot for Bigfoot beasts. There is at least one reported sighting here, so we decided to check it out. We stayed there for a few hours that day and felt watched and followed the whole time. I took various photographs throughout the investigation and, when I checked back through them, I spotted the creepy picture. It looks like a shadowy figure [standing] within the trees, staring at us from afar. It shows something dark, a different colour against all that greenery."

He also added, however: "I make no bold claims, but my fellow investigators think this could be genuine evidence that the British Bigfoot exists… These creatures are seen all over the UK, and the phenomenon spreads from Scotland right down to southern England. These people are clearly seeing something, and that something cannot be passed off as simply hoaxes or known animals. This is something unknown."

Debbie Crossley Hatswell, one of British Bigfoot Research team members, also claims she saw the creature at close range when she was fifteen, describing the creature as having an ape-like physique, a mouth the same as a human's, a huge jaw, and dark, tanned, weathered skin covered in dark brown hair.

Without doubt, the English countryside, for all its majestic beauty, can be a frightening place. After all, who has not found themselves alone at night in a forest and had strange thoughts and irrational fears running through their head? And in this case, maybe, just maybe, something large and hairy is running around and making its presence known to the public. Whatever is going on— if anything—it is extremely strange, to say the very least.

Chapter Six

A Talking Mongoose, the Devil's Footprints, and the
Curious Case of Spring-heeled Jack

If vampires in Scottish castles or hairy men in lush forests aren't strange enough, then let us consider the next story—one that has defied explanation for over ninety years and reportedly happened in the early 1930s in a farmhouse known as Cashen's Gap, near the hamlet of Dalby on the Isle of Man.

In September 1931, James Irving, his wife Margaret and their daughter Voirrey, began to hear strange noises in the attic of their farmhouse. Before long these scratching and rustling sounds could also be heard behind the wood-panelled walls of the house. Initially, they thought it was a rat, but then the unseen creature began making different sounds, at times sounding like a ferret or growling like a dog. At times it even gurgled like a baby, in a similar way to a baby learning to speak. Soon the voice began to parrot words that the family often used, and in a very short space of time appeared as if it had effectively learned to speak English.

The unseen creature then shocked the family by introducing itself as Gef, a mongoose. It claimed to have been born in New Delhi, India, in 1852 and, according to Voirrey—apparently the only person who ever saw him properly—Gef was the size of a rat, with yellowish fur and a large bushy tail. Interestingly, an Indian mongoose is actually much larger than a rat and does not have a bushy tail.

Nevertheless, Gef claimed to be clever, as well as being an earthbound spirit and a ghost in the form of a weasel. He was reported to have said: "I am a freak. I have hands, and I have feet, and if you saw me, you'd faint, you'd be petrified, mummified, turned into stone or a pillar of salt."

As well as talking, Gef could also sing, and he apparently knew the words to many popular songs. As well, he appeared to have a sense of humour and provided the family with an interesting source of entertainment. However, it has been said that he sometimes took his practical joking too far: indeed, one time pretending to have been poisoned, which worried the family immensely.

Annoyingly, Gef insisted on remaining hidden, except for occasionally showing himself fleetingly to Voirrey. He apparently lived within the walls of the house but would often venture into the garden. In reality, the only evidence that the creature existed was the sound of his voice and a number of other strange happenings, such as objects being moved and thrown about the house, characteristics usually ascribed to poltergeist activity.

At one stage Margaret Irving managed to stroke Gef's fur through a hole in a wall. Unfortunately, she cut her finger on his sharp teeth. Showing concern for her well-being, Gef immediately instructed her to go and put ointment on the wound.

All in all, it appears that the strange mongoose entity was friendly, funny and sensitive, although he could lose his temper. In addition, he was frisky and sometimes a little accident-prone. On one occasion his antics were apparently too much for the family, who threatened to move out, which apparently upset the creature, who seemed to love the company and was afraid that he would be left on his own. When the family decided to stay, he became much more obedient and promised not to be so lively.

It was reported that Gef would often venture out of the house and wander around the island. He would apparently spy on other people and report back to the Irvings on local happenings. Occasionally, some of the locals reported hearing the odd sounds of an invisible creature, which they believed to be the Irvings' pet mongoose.

Interestingly, in 1912 a farmer who owned some mongooses released them, hoping that they would reduce the population of rabbits on the island as they were becoming a pest. Is it possible that some of these mongooses survived and bred? Could one of these have been the smooth-talking Gef?

Before long the improbable story of Gef the talking mongoose reached the popular press, and the story became a great favourite at the time, with scores of journalists making the boat trip to the island to either see or hear the elusive little creature. With all this publicity, the happenings soon came to the attention of paranormal investigators, and in July 1935 Richard S. Lambert, editor of *The Listener*, and Harry Price, renowned ghost hunter, went to the Isle of Mann to investigate.

Price set out to conduct a proper scientific study of the Irvings' farmhouse, with the aim of obtaining conclusive evidence as to the existence of the mysterious mongoose. However, the research was unsuccessful, and Price himself never managed to even catch a glimpse of the animal. Apart from this, the evidence produced was very weak, consisting of a few blurry photographs of something that bore a remarkable resemblance to a cat, as well as some strange hairs that were not dissimilar to those of the Irvings' dog.

Nevertheless, Price and Lambert were unperturbed, and next year published a book about the case, called *The Haunting of Cashen's Gap*. The book itself was described as "an essay in the Veracious but Unaccountable" but, in reality, was more of a lighthearted story than serious research. Tellingly, both Price and Lambert refused to say whether they believed the story or not but noted that it must be viewed with an open mind.

Price did manage, however, to get some paw prints and tooth marks in plasticine, apparently made by Gef. These were sent to the British Natural History Museum where, oddly enough, a curator could not match them to any known animal, although he did concede that they were not made by a mongoose and could have conceivably been made by a small dog.

But Harry Price was not the only researcher to take an interest in the case: Nandor Fodor, a leading authority on poltergeists and all kinds of paranormal phenomena, also decided to examine the strange tales. Fodor stayed at the Irvings' house for a week but unfortunately neither heard nor saw Gef. However, he interviewed both the family and the locals and was utterly convinced that what he had heard was true. He stated that he found the Irvings to be "sincere, frank and simple", and that "deliberate deception on the part of the whole family cannot be entertained as a solution of the mystery".

Interestingly, Fodor came to the conclusion that Gef was not a poltergeist, as none of the family members were psychic and Gef had never shown any real paranormal powers. He also noted that Gef had been seen, photographed and touched, and claimed to be a small furry animal.

In 1937 the Irvings had to sell the farm and move. Reportedly, they accepted a lower offer on it as it was reputed to be haunted. What happened to Gef is not known, although many believe he simply followed the family to their new home. This, however, has never been verified.

In 1946 the new owner of the farm, Leslie Graham, claimed that he had shot and killed Gef. However, when later put on display, the creature was black and white and apparently much larger than the talkative little mongoose. Voirrey Irving, who saw the dead creature, was certain that it was not Gef. Whatever the case, Price's own conclusion was that Gef was a fantasy, probably like an imaginary friend, that provided entertainment and interest for the Irving family. However, Voirrey Irving, in an interview published late in her life, maintained that he was real and not a creation of her imagination.

But if mongooses can apparently talk and sing, then what can we make of the next strange story, that of the Devil's footprints??

The night of the 8 February 1855 saw a heavy snowfall on the small villages and countryside of southern Devon. The last snow was believed to have fallen around midnight, and between this time and early the following morning something, it appeared, had left an innumerable number of strange tracks in the snow. These tracks stretched for over a hundred miles and it was reported that the impressions closely resembled that of a donkey's shoe, and measured from an inch and a half to two and a half inches across and appeared to be cloven.

The tracks, or footprints as they were known, were hoof-shaped and, remarkably, passed over rooftops, through walls, and covered huge areas of land. One set of the prints were reported as straddling a two-mile-wide span of the River Exe, continuing on the other side as if the creature had simply walked over the water. In some cases, they went through solid walls and haystacks, appearing on the other side as though there were no barrier whatsoever.

Some of the prints stopped abruptly and then continued after lengthy breaks. Others stopped at walls as high as fourteen feet, only to continue on the other side, leaving untouched snow on the top of the wall, as if the creature had simply walked straight through the wall. Some prints were recorded as travelling through narrow openings such as drainpipes. In some cases, it seemed that whatever it was had walked up to a front door and then decided against going in and had walked away.

It soon became clear that the phenomenon was widespread; indeed, it seemed that most of south Devon was exposed to the occurrence. The prints were examined in great detail by scientists and naturalists alike, with the distance between the steps found to be a uniform eight and a half inches. This spacing was consistent wherever the tracks were measured. Also noted was the way in which the prints were set out, one in front of the other, which suggested a biped rather than a quadruped (a four-legged animal).

The clergy soon pronounced their position, declaring them to be those of the devil who, they suggested, was roaming the night in search of sinners. Whereas this theory was rejected as ridiculous superstition, there remained a feeling of unease and fear in the population. After all, no one as yet had actually been able to explain the marks. The devil's footprints seemed as good as an explanation as there could be.

Although the marks did not reappear, the national press soon got hold of the story, which brought the whole issue to national prominence and led to some incredible speculation by eminent scientists and laymen alike. One theory was that some kangaroos had escaped from a nearby private zoo, which seemed a reasonable theory—except that the prints were nothing like those of a kangaroo, and kangaroos generally don't walk straight through walls or cover distances of a hundred miles on freezing nights in the snow.

A biologist, Sir Richard Owen, put forward the premise that the tracks were made by badgers whilst wandering around looking for food. The strange prints, he suggested, were the result of the prints thawing then refreezing. This theory, however, held as much credence as all the others, which included roaming racoons, rats, swans, otters, freak atmospheric conditions, and—bizarrely—a hot air balloon passing over head trailing a rope. Whereas these could explain *some* of the tracks, they certainly could not explain all of them: the uniformity of the tracks was apparently quite incredible.

The extent of the footprints was most probably vastly exaggerated. However, there is no doubt that they existed and were extensive. Whatever they were remains a complete mystery today and will probably remain so, unless the exact same conditions are presented where they can be more closely examined and scientifically studied.

But if authorities and others had absolutely no idea what it was that went walking through Devon on that freezing February night in 1855, we do know what it was that terrorised London in the early to mid-1800s, even if it defies explanation.

Spring-heeled Jack first made his presence known in London in 1837, with the last reported sighting being in Liverpool as late as 1904. The first report of this peculiar and genuinely frightening creature was when a businessman, returning home late one night from work, was shocked when a mysterious figure jumped over the high railings of Barnes Cemetery and landed in front of him. Although there was no attack, the description of the entity was somewhat disturbing, a muscular man with devilish features, including large and pointed ears and nose, and protruding, glowing eyes.

Later, in October 1837, Mary Stevens, a servant girl, was walking to Lavender Hill after visiting her parents in Battersea. While crossing Clapham Common, a figure leapt at her from a dark alley, grabbing her and kissing her face while at the same time ripping off her clothes and touching her with what she described as claws, but "cold and clammy as those of a corpse". Terrified, she screamed, which seemed to scare the attacker off. The screaming also attracted the attention a number of residents but, although they immediately started searching for the attacker, nothing was found.

The very next day the enigmatic figure resurfaced, this time by bounding in the path of a carriage causing the coachman to lose control and crash. Witnesses then claimed that the figure escaped by jumping clear over a nine-foot-high wall while emitting an unearthly high-pitched laugh.

To put it all in context, in the early nineteenth century there were numerous reports of ghosts who stalked the gloomy, crime-ridden streets of London. These figures were described as pale and human-like and apparently preyed on lone pedestrians. Indeed, in 1803, one of these ghosts was reported to have grabbed a woman who was walking past Hammersmith chapel. Apparently, she later died from the shock. Another ghoul, the so-called Southampton ghost, was also reported as roaming the streets at night and assaulting individuals. Intriguingly, he was reported as being over ten feet high and able to jump over houses.

And so, it was in this environment of Victorian England that the attacker came to prominence, and before long the news of the character spread. The press and the public, eager for scandal and a bit of horror, soon dubbed him Spring-heeled Jack.

He was described as having a terrifying and frightful appearance, and struck genuine fear into the hearts of the residents of Victorian London. Witnesses told stories of clawed hands, and eyes that resembled red balls of burning coal or fire. One report suggested that beneath his black cloak he wore a helmet and a tight-fitting piece of clothing, somewhat similar to an oilskin.

Many others reported him as being devil-like in appearance, although, oddly, others described him as having the appearance of a gentleman. Several witnesses spoke of his ability to breathe blue and white flames, and others suggested that his claws were, in fact, metallic gloves with artificial claws. Interestingly, like the Southampton ghost, he was also described as very tall and thin. One report even suggested that he looked like a bear.

Whatever the case, the attacks and sightings increased, to the point that the Lord Mayor of London, Sir John Cowan, revealed an anonymous letter suggesting that the whole things was a fake, and that someone from "the highest ranks of life" had taken a wager for the "task of visiting many of the villages near London in three different disguises, a ghost, a bear and a devil".

Although Cowan was sceptical about the letter, it was later confirmed that servant girls in Kensington, Hammersmith and Ealing had been telling stories of the ghost or devil. The matter was soon reported to *The Times,* and it seemed at this stage as if the legend of Spring-heeled Jack was no more than that of a bored, upper-class hoaxer.

However, on reporting in *The Times*, a flood of letter was received, some deriding the so-called hoaxer and others reporting that several more women had been attacked in Hammersmith, some suffering serious wounds. Another writer to the newspaper stoked the fires of hysteria by claiming that several people had died of fright, while others had suffered serious fits after being attacked by the ghastly creature.

Cowan remained sceptical but kept an open mind. He believed that, although it could all be a hoax, there was still a chance that something supernatural was happening. Indeed, a servant girl whom he apparently trusted told him that she had been scared into having fits by a figure dressed in a bearskin. As a result, Cowan decided to act, and the police were given instructions to find the person or persons responsible.

In April 1838, a gardener in Rosehill, Sussex, reported that he had been terrified by a creature that appeared to be like a bear, which, after growling at him, then climbed a garden wall and ran along it on all fours before jumping down and chasing him. It then scaled the wall and disappeared. Surprisingly, *The Times* concluded that Spring-heeled Jack had somehow found his way to the Sussex coast, although the report bore absolutely no resemblance to other accounts of attacks.

The most infamous of attacks, however, occurred in February 1838 when two young girls, Jane Alsop and Lucy Scales, were assaulted in separate incidents some eight days apart. The reporting of these two cases, especially in *The Times*, greatly raised the profile of Spring-heeled Jack.

On the night of the 19 February, Jane Alsop answered the door of her family home to find a man claiming to be a police officer. He ordered her to bring a torch, claiming that he had caught Spring-heeled Jack. She quickly found a candle and handed it to the man, who suddenly threw off his cloak and spewed blue and white flames in her face. She also reported that his eyes resembled red balls of fire and that he wore a large helmet and what appeared to be a tight-fitting white oilskin.

Then, without a word, he began tearing at her gown with his claws, which she later said may have been made of some metallic substance. As she screamed for help, she ran back into the house, but he followed, clawing at her neck and arms until one of her sisters, upon hearing the screams, intervened. Spring-heeled Jack then fled into the night.

Eight days later, on the 28 February, eighteen-year-old Lucy Scales and her sister were returning home after visiting their brother, a butcher who lived in the London borough of Tower Hamlets. As the two girls passed along Green Dragon Alley, they saw a person standing in the passage. Lucy, who was walking in front of her sister at the time, approached the person, who was wearing a large cloak. At that point he turned to her and spurted what she described as "a quantity of blue flame" in her face. Temporarily blinded, she fell to the ground and suffered a violent fit, which apparently lasted for a number of hours.

Her brother, having heard her screams, came to her assistance. He found Lucy on the ground, having a fit, with her sister attempting to help her. Lucy was quickly transported home, and the sister later reported that the assailant had been tall, thin, and of a gentlemanly appearance, covered in a large cloak and carrying a small lamp, similar to those used by the police. After the attack he apparently just walked away and, although the police questioned a number of people, no one was ever convicted of the attack.

Intriguingly, immediately after the attack on Jane Alsop, a man by the name of Thomas Millbank was arrested after boasting that *he* was Spring-heeled Jack. He was tried at Lambeth Street Court, and during the trial it was revealed that he had been wearing white overalls and a greatcoat, which he dropped outside the Alsop house. A candle, believed to be the one given to Spring-heeled Jack by Jane, was also found. However, Millbank escaped conviction because Jane Alsop insisted her attacker had breathed fire, and Millbank could obviously do no such thing.

Although now a household name—indeed, his exploits were reported in the newspapers, serialised in a number of 'Penny Dreadfuls' and even performed as cheap plays—Spring-heeled Jack's appearances started to wane. However, in 1843 a number of sightings were reported from Northamptonshire to East Anglia, where there were rumours of attacks on drivers of mail coaches. Indeed, he was even tenuously linked with the phenomenon of the Devil's Footprints.

A couple of years later, in 1845, Spring-heeled Jack was again sighted, this time in West London, leaping over hedges and walls and laughing demonically. However, unlike the Jack of old, this one was soon caught and turned out to be a hoaxer. However, hoaxer or not, the legend of Spring-heeled Jack refused to die, and things were soon to take a grisly course when, in November 1845, the fire-breathing figure confronted a thirteen-year-old prostitute named Maria Davies in Bermondsey. He breathed fire into her face and then threw her unconscious body into a water-filled ditch, where she drowned.

But this was not the last of Spring-heeled Jack: throughout the 1850s and 1860s he was seen all over England, leaping over fences and walls and springing between rooftops. Indeed, so prevalent was his legend and infamy that people stayed off the streets at night, or at least stayed in well-lit and populated areas. Vigilante groups were formed to patrol the streets at night, and the police formed extra patrols to search for the terrifying creature. Still, all of this came to nothing: every time he was sighted, he simply bounded away with unearthly physical prowess, leaving nothing but ungodly laughter in the ears of his would-be captors.

In August 1877 he appeared at Aldershot Barracks, where he leapt up and slapped the face of a surprised and terrified sentry. Apparently, the soldier observed a figure advancing towards him and issued a challenge. The figure continued to advance and then rapidly delivered several slaps to the soldier's face. After recovering from the shock, the soldier fired at him, but with no visible effect. It has been suggested that the soldier was either so shaken that his aim was bad or that he was issued with blanks—either way, Spring-heeled Jack appeared unhurt and disappeared back into the darkness through a series of incredibly large bounds.

Forty-five years later, a memoir written by Lord Ernest Hamilton, a soldier and conservative politician from 1885 to 1892, mentioned the appearance of Spring-heeled Jack at the Aldershot Barracks. Although he suggested the event may have happened in 1879, he added that there were numerous instances where the same sort of thing happened and, as a result, there was a great deal of panic around the sightings, and sentries were issued live ammunition and ordered to shoot whatever it was if it reappeared. Suspiciously, after the orders to shoot on sight were given, the appearances ceased, which suggested that it was all an elaborate prank. Hamilton himself believed that it was carried out by one of his fellow officers, a Lieutenant Alfrey, although nothing could be proven.

Another sighting of Jack was reported in autumn

1877, this time at Newport Arch in Lincoln, Lincolnshire, and he was rumoured to be wearing a sheepskin. In this instance a mob chased and cornered him before shooting at him. However, as in Aldershot the bullets apparently had no effect, and he simply bounded away.

But Spring-heeled Jack's days were now numbered, and he was last reported in Liverpool in September of 1904, jumping on rooftops. A few weeks later he was seen scaling the steeple of a church, before disappearing with his customary large leaps behind a row of houses.

Although there have been later reports of a similar character, it is believed that the 1904 sighting was the last. Having said this, in south Herefordshire in 1986 a travelling salesman claimed to have had an encounter with a creature similar to Spring-heeled Jack. The man apparently leapt in enormous bounds and passed the salesman on the road, slapping his cheek as he did so. The salesman later described his clothing as similar to a black ski suit. He also noted that the man had an elongated chin. Maybe Spring-heeled Jack had somehow transcended time itself and was on the loose again?

Apart from Thomas Millbank, no one was ever identified as Spring-heeled Jack. His extraordinary ability to escape and the long period of time in which he operated has led to all sorts of strange theories about his nature and identity, and while most people seek to explain his exploits in rational terms, others have explored the more spectacular details in light of the whole thing having a supernatural element.

It has been suggested that the whole thing was simply a case of mass hysteria, brought on by sensational reporting in the popular press, as well as a general unease at the state of Victorian London in terms of safety to the public. And as we saw with the Devil's Footprints and the Cottingley fairies, Victorian society, for all its new-found scientific knowledge, was not above superstition.

Others have suggested that a number of different individuals may have been behind the events, and this spawned a copycat-like environment, which allowed Jack to prosper over such a long period of time—indeed, much longer than one would expect for someone so incredibly athletic. In this sense, Spring-heeled Jack could be seen not as a supernatural creature but rather one or more people with a macabre sense of humour. A popular idea at the time attributed the attacks to the Marquis of Waterford, but this was never proven.

On the paranormal side, a wide range of highly speculative paranormal explanations have been proposed. These include Spring-heeled Jack being an extraterrestrial entity with superhuman agility, obtained as a result of living on a high-gravity world, or that he was a demon, somehow summoned into the world by occult practitioners or witches. Some even speculated that, as in Devon in 1855, he was the devil himself.

Whatever the case, the Victorian age was one that abounded with new scientific theories. Superstition was being relegated to the realms of folklore due to new advances in science, medicine, and chemistry. Theories such as Charles Darwin's theory of evolution or

Wallace's similar thesis about evolution and natural selection were difficult for some people to accept, especially those who could not believe that humans had descended from apes. Some of those who dismissed Darwin's ideas may have been involved in elaborate hoaxes as a way of disproving evolution. Of course, it could have just as easily been some practical jokers who wanted to make a name for themselves by scaring the wits out of Londoners by wearing strange costumes.

Whatever the case, Spring-heeled Jack will forever be remembered as one of the stranger stories to ever emerge from England and the British Isles themselves.

But if a talking mongoose, the devil's footsteps, and bloodcurdling, leaping ghoul are not strange enough, then what of the alleged cryptid sighted in the 1970s in the village of Mawnan, Cornwall? And this is something we shall look at in the next chapter, where things are almost too weird for words.

Chapter Seven

Too Weird for Words?

Cornwall, as we have seen in previous chapters, is an ancient and forbidding landscape that hides many strange and unexplainable secrets. It is a place of bleak, windswept moors and craggy sea-swept coasts. A place that is thought to harbour piskies and mermaids and many other weird and wonderful creatures. And yet, for all this, it is doubtful that any are stranger than the extremely weird reports of the Owlman of Mawnan.

The Cornish Owlman, or Owlman of Mawnan, is a bizarre cryptid that was allegedly sighted in and around the village of Mawnan during the mid-1970s. And, like other strange phenomena of a similar ilk, it is hard to categorise it as supernatural, imagination, or misinterpretation. Interestingly, the creature only appeared in one specific place, for a very short period of time, and there is no body of folklore surrounding it. As such, it could have been easily dismissed—were it not for the curious circumstances surrounding it.

Whatever the case, the Owlman was reported during the years 1976 to 1978, in the vicinity of the Mawnan Village. These sightings were reported to a well-known paranormal researcher by the name of Tony Shiels, who reputedly coined the name of the strange creature.

From reported sightings, the Owlman appeared to be a particularly strange hybrid that combined human and owl anatomy. Its size was said to be that of an average person, and it was often seen flying, which rules out the possibility of a hoaxer in a costume. It reputedly made a loud hissing noise and had glowing red eyes, while its claws were unusually large and black in colour. The feathers were generally described as owl-like and light grey or white. It was purportedly sighted by many witnesses in Mawnan Woods and in the cemetery of Mawnan, and strangely seemed to appear more often than not to young girls.

In 1976 Shiels was approached by a man by the name of Don Melling, who was on holiday with his family in Cornwall. He stated to Shiels that on 17 April of that year his two daughters were walking through the woods near Mawnan Church when they saw a large winged creature hovering above the church tower. Frightened by this, the girls ran off to tell their father and, as a result of the sighting, the family was perturbed enough to cut short their holiday. Interestingly, Melling would not let his daughters be interviewed, although he did allow Shiels to have a drawing of the creature, made by June, the elder of the two.

Then, in early July, another young girl, Sally Chapman, was camping with a friend in the woods near the church when she heard a hissing sound and was alarmed to see a figure that looked like an owl with pointed ears and red eyes but as big as a man. The girls reported that the creature flew up into the air, revealing black pincer-like claws. On the following day there were more reported sightings of the creature.

Previous to this encounter, Chapman and her friend

had read a pamphlet that described the Owlman's previous appearance in April 1976. They contacted Shiels, who suggested that they draw separate images of what they saw. Shiels considered them similar enough to verify their story but different enough to rule out conspiracy.

Then, in 1989, a young man called Gavin claimed to see the creature when he and his girlfriend witnessed a five -foot-tall creature with feet that were large and black, with two huge toes. The creature was grey and brown, with glowing eyes, and reminded them of a giant owl.

Overall, there were several sightings of the Owlman between 1976 and 1978, all in the vicinity of Mawnan Church, but these sighting appeared to stop just as quickly as they appeared. However, in 1995, a female tourist from Chicago wrote a letter to the *Western Morning News* in Truro, claiming to have seen a "man bird with a ghastly face, a wide mouth, glowing eyes and pointed ears," as well as having "clawed wings".

Although an interesting story in its own right, Cornwall at this particular time seemed to be plagued with unusual phenomena, including numerous sightings of sea monsters, ghostly apparitions, and animals behaving in strange ways—including dogs, cats, and birds attacking people for no apparent reason. In addition, there was a huge increase in UFO sightings in the area. It must be noted that, in the spring of 1976, the weather in Cornwall was going through extreme shifts between unusual heatwaves and cold snaps, and this may have contributed to the strange behaviour of animals.

However, whatever the cause, it does appear that something strange was happening in the area at the time.

Having said that, what exactly *was* Owlman? Given that there seemed to be a lot of unusual occurrences in Cornwall at the time, it is easy to suggest that some form of mass hysteria could be responsible for the sightings. Of course, something really strange may have actually been happening, such as a freak form of weather or energy, which could help explain the peaks in temperatures that spring.

A logical explanation is that sightings of the Owlman were nothing more than that of an escaped eagle-owl, a species that can grow to quite an enormous size—indeed, up to two feet tall—with a wingspan of nearly six feet. And as I have been present when an eagle-owl has been flying, I can tell you that they are very huge and impressive birds. Indeed, one sighting of the Owlman in the late 1980s described it as being four feet high, with two large toes on the front of each foot, and it ducked down and forwards before it took off. This is consistent with a large owl, as is the arrangement of the toes. However, this still doesn't quite explain the sightings of man-owl hybrids so it would seem the legend of Owlman will continue for quite some time into the future.

Interestingly, Ron Halliday, in his book *Edinburgh After Dark*, noted something similar to the Owlman sightings, retelling the following tale: "In October 1992, in a house overlooking Niddry Burn, a woman only known as Moira woke up in the early hours of the morning and caught sight of an intense white light, clearly visible through the window. She got out of bed to take a closer look, and her attention was drawn to a tree at the foot of the garden. Crouching on a thick branch was a creature, which she took at first to be a giant bird, one as big as a man. Moira was frightened and fascinated all at the same time. She wanted to step back from the window, but felt a powerful influence, as if she were unable to look away. But, as she took a longer look, she became aware that apart from its huge size there were other strange aspects to it. It seemed to have a mixture of human and bird-type features: ordinary arms and legs, but attached to its back were two large wings. It was a disturbing experience, although the entity did not seem aware of her presence and made no attempt to confront her. Oddly, Moira's husband slept through her sighting and couldn't be woken up. Moira too, felt 'a bit strange', almost as if she had 'walked into another world'."

And while we're on the subject of winged anomalies, we should quickly examine reports of winged snakes in the woodlands surrounding Penllyne Castle in Glamorgan. According to witnesses, local farmers often shot the creatures, as they believed they posed a threat to their chickens.

One witness, whose recollections were recorded in 1909, noted: "Some of them had crests sparkling with all the colours of the rainbow. When disturbed, they glided swiftly, sparkling all over, to their lairs. When angry, they flew over people's heads, with outspread wings bright, and sometimes with eyes too, like the feathers in a peacock's tail."

One elderly woman said the woods close to Porthkerry Park were infested with winged snakes and that her grandfather had killed one and kept its feathered skin. After the grandfather died, however, it was discarded.

So, what on earth are we actually talking about here? Is it possible that the so-called winged snakes existed? Were they some relic from the past that suggested that dragons, however implausible it sounds, actually existed? Certainly, it would appear in the minds of some that they did. Or are we are simply misinterpreting what was seen?

Some facts about these bizarre creatures stand out, including the feathered skin from one of these flying serpents, which was kept by one family for many years. This suggests that, rather than being reptilian, that the creatures were, in fact, birds. However, if we are to conclude this, we must also realise that birds have descended from dinosaurs, which suddenly puts the flying snakes back in a different light.

Another feature is that these creatures could sometimes be seen seeming 'coiled up', which is a trait of a number of long-necked birds. In addition, these flying serpents were often said to have clawed feet, and the claws—strangely enough, and unlike any bird in existence—were also said to be poisonous. Is it possible, however remote the possibility, that the Welsh flying snakes were in fact wyverns, the mythological two-legged and winged dragon?

Whatever the case, Owlmen, angel-like creatures, and flying snakes are not the only extremely strange creatures that continue to pop up and amaze people in the United Kingdom. Indeed, sometimes it would appear that non-flying snakes also exist: not vipers and other small indigenous British snakes, but snakes of immense length. And once again, we find these extraordinary reports come from an area seemingly overrun by strange creatures: Cannock Chase.

In May 2009 a rambler, walking through the chase, reported seeing a python-sized creature near the German Cemetery and described it as brightly coloured with a powerful head. However, this is not the first time that incredulous witnesses have reported seeing such improbable creatures. Paranormal investigator Nick Redfern believes it's probably a monster mutant, and may have links with the Loch Ness Monster.

In March, 2006, the *Birmingham Post* ran an article reporting the sighting of a fourteen-foot snake moving through bracken near Birches Valley, stating that "[t]he beast had a powerful head and colouring that stood out sharply against the greens and blues of the bracken".

Previously, in the summer of 1976, Norman Dodd had an even more bizarre encounter. In a subsequent interview with Redfern, Dodd said he spotted the enormous snake in a small millpond noting that "[i]t was a bloody stifling day. I remember swigging something to drink and having a bite when there was something moving on the bank."

Dodd was then astonished to see a seven-foot-long creature surface from the water and then bask on the edge of the pool: "It sort of wriggled. It was like its whole body seemed to sort of shake and wobble as it moved. I know it saw me—or saw the car, definitely—because it looked right in this direction and then went back to what it was up to, just lying there."

Redfern has stated: "Dodd's eye-opening report was one of those that almost sounded too good to be true—and yet the wholly independent story of a giant snake seen in the Cannock Chase woods in early 2006 suggested to me that such Loch Ness Monster-like beasts were indeed on the loose in the area—and, perhaps, they still are…"

However, as much as we would like to think that some sort of relative of the Loch Ness Monster is lurking in the woods of Cannock Chase, it is much easier to simply suggest that these large snakes are just that: pythons, a popular pet, that may have escaped or been dumped by their owners once it grew to an enormous length. Having said that, one would suspect that a python would surely die in the chilly winter months, and yet the reports keep emerging.

But giant snakes are not the only reptiles that keep appearing: in February 2014, a bus driver, Jolyon Rea, flagged down a passing police officer and informed her that he'd seen a six-foot-long crocodile swimming under Bedminster Bridge in the River Avon, not far from the city centre of Bristol. Police immediately searched the area but could find nothing.

In another sighting, a forty-one-year-old woman said

she was threatened by the crocodile that was walking along a road, and a local councillor, Tom Aditya, even managed to take some video footage of a six-foot-long creature moving slowly along the river, terrifying water birds as it did.

In June 2014, Tamara Blanco, of Southville, Bristol, said she had been jogging close to the Clifton suspension bridge when she saw something lurking in the water. She commented that she "felt scared at the time because the thing—whatever it was—was moving in the water. I wanted to stay to see it properly, but there was no one around and I just didn't feel comfortable." She added: "[I] could feel my hair start to stand on end and I thought, 'Oh my God, is it a crocodile?' and I just left the place."

Dr Ian Stephen, a reptile and amphibian expert, said crocodiles and alligators could survive in British waters, pointing out that alligators can live through cold US winters, although pointing out that if it was a crocodile then it would have to have either escaped or been released from captivity. Benjamin Tapley, team leader of herpetology at London Zoo, said alligators were more likely to survive British waters than crocodiles and that, although a crocodile *could* survive, it certainly couldn't flourish due to the cold-water temperatures in the rivers.

But it's not just out-of-place reptiles that concern us as, in August 2012, a man and a woman claimed they saw a lion sitting in a field in Essex. Police were dispatched to search, along with experts from Colchester Zoo—but there was no sign of the beast.

And with that, we have just about wrapped up our voyage of discovery through mysterious creatures of the British Isles—except, that is, for a few final stories, some of which are so bizarre and outlandish that it may just make the reader believe in all the creatures we have previously examined.

On 1 April 2011, the *Liverpool Echo* published a story about a creature so strange and, in fact, frightening, that it completely defies any explanation.

Staff at the North West Water Company United Utilities were said to be terrified when closed-circuit cameras captured an image of a hideous humanoid creature in the sewers. The creature, which was filmed by engineers, can clearly be seen standing upright on its back legs, and has what appears to be exceptionally long, thick arms, a round face, and large glowing eyes. It is believed the animal managed to survive by eating fat deposits within Merseyside's sewer pipes. Indeed, Ian Appleton, who was operating the CCTV unit at the time of the sighting, said: "I physically jumped when I saw the thing."

Mike Wood, network manager at the company, suggested that "the animal could possibly be a domestic pet or, feasibly, an animal that has escaped from the zoo," while others have dubbed the weird humanoid creature 'Messie', likening it to a dirty version of the Loch Ness Monster.

However, Dr Pauline Yorleg, a Liverpool lecturer specialising in sewage sightings, put everything into perspective by dismissively stating: "I've not been this excited since red herrings were found in Wallasey last April."

But if the bizarre sewer creature of Liverpool is beyond comprehension, then what of our next curious report, that of the walking fir cone of Dumpton Park?

Although reports are scarce, it appears that on 16 April 1954, one Police Constable Bishop was walking through Dumpton Park in Ramsgate, Kent, when he encountered a bizarre animal that he described as "a walking fir cone". Since this encounter, nothing more has been heard of the creature. However, is it possible that Bishop had encountered a scaly anteater or pangolin that had somehow escaped from a nearby zoo? Although there were no records of such an escapee, the pangolin is nothing if not pine cone-like, with its strange bulbous scales and odd gait.

Whatever the case, we shall never know, although, being Australian, I am well aware of a common lizard that resides in this country: the shingleback skink (*Trachydosaurus rugosus*), commonly known as a 'Stumpy Tail'. These harmless little lizards possess short, stumpy tails, which are brown in colour with large scales and look remarkably like a pine or fir cone on legs. Maybe Bishop had come across one of these placid lizards, although it is hard to see how he could have mistaken it for a pine cone and not a lizard. Again, we shall never know.

But whereas our last mystery creature could have

simply been due to misidentification of an existing exotic species, the next is not so clear-cut. In fact, although one may be able to make a number of suggestions as to what it was, there still remains some element of doubt as the reader will soon see.

One of Britain's most grisly mystery beasts must be the earth hound, or yard pig, of Banffshire in northern Scotland, which—gruesomely—is said to live in or near graveyards and digs inside coffins to feed on corpses. It has been described as being "something between a rat and a weasel, and about the size of a ferret, head very like that of a dog, the tail was not very long. At a casual glance it would be mistaken for a rat, but was quite unlike on close examination."

Alexander Fenton and Scottish cryptozoologist David Heppell have discovered a number of intriguing accounts regarding this strange creature, including one written in 1917 by a Mr A. Smith, documenting the description of an earth hound by a gardener who had accidentally managed to kill one about half a century earlier while ploughing some fields near a churchyard. According to the gardener, it was brown in colour and had a long, hound-like head, as well as a bushy tail.

Another earth hound was apparently killed around 1915 near Mastrick, again near a churchyard, and was said to have mole-like feet, white tusks, and prominent pig-like nostrils. As noted, most sightings of this odd little creature appear to be when it is accidentally dug up by a plough or a gardener or found in a graveyard. And given the morbid habits it appears to have—that is, feeding on corpses—it is likely to be nothing more than superstition, although one must note that moles and badgers would definitely be attracted to the worms and beetles associated with buried corpses. Having said that, it is difficult to understand how a gardener could mistake a badger or a mole for a completely different and unknown creature.

And while on the subject of badger-like creatures, our next mystery beast may have some of the characteristics of the earth hound, except that it is to be found in the Mendips in England rather than the cool climes of northern Scotland and seems to possess some sort of supernatural powers, as experienced by the warden of the Charterhouse Centre, an ex-Royal Marine called Terry, who had a perplexing and terrifying encounter while staying at the centre.

Terry was described as being a man who had excellent leadership qualities and was not prone to flights of fancy. As an ex-Royal Marine, he was tough and well-disciplined, which makes this next story even odder.

The Charterhouse Centre, as well as being an educational institute, was also used by the Mendip Cave Rescue team as a store for their equipment. As such, Terry, being a member of the rescue team, was at the centre alone one night cleaning and checking rescue gear and, realising that he had a lot of work to do, phoned his wife to inform her that he would stay overnight in the centre rather than drive home.

At about 10.00 p.m. he decided to finish working on

the equipment, made a bowl of soup and watched some television. After a while he decided to go to bed, and so grabbed a sleeping bag and headed off to the sick bay, where he fell asleep on the bunk with his back to the door and facing the outside wall.

Sometime around 1.00 a.m., he was woken by an odd snuffling noise from outside, something that reminded him of an animal, possibly a badger rustling around in the leaves and grass. He dropped off to sleep again but was surprised when he was again woken by the noise—except this time it was no longer coming from outside the building but downstairs within the hall.

Terry was convinced that he had closed and locked the doors but couldn't be bothered getting up and checking, so he decided to not worry about it, figuring that if an animal had found its way in then surely it could find its way out again. However, as he lay there, he could hear the animal getting closer—in fact, ascending the stairs and snuffling and scratching around on the landing outside the closed door to the sick bay. This time, Terry was somewhat alarmed, as it is rare for an animal to explore so deep into the building. For some reason, he recalled that he felt threatened by the sound.

The snuffling continued, and Terry lay there wondering what it could be. Then, to his horror, it sounded as if it were trying to squeeze under the door of the room, something that was impossible: the gap between the door and floor was only half an inch. Terry froze as the sound continued, somewhat like a stiff brush being pushed under the door. It then somehow managed to enter the room under the door before falling silent. Whatever it was, it was apparent that it was now in the pitch-black room.

Then the sound of the snuffling and scratching started up again, this time immediately behind him—in fact, only inches away from his back. His body was frozen in terror as the noise continued. Terrifyingly, the bed then started violently rocking, so much so that the ex-Royal Marine had to grab onto it so as not to be thrown off.

And then, after thirty seconds, the jerking and thrusting of the bed stopped, and Terry lay there exhausted. As he did, he heard the snuffling and scratching noise make its way from the bedside back towards the door. Then the creature once again dragged itself under the door and descended the stairs before disappearing outside.

Terry lay there for a while, in complete silence, before glancing at his watch, which showed 2.00 a.m. The creature had apparently been there for a whole hour, and although intrigued by what it was, he was simply too frightened to open the door and go down the stairs to find out. Instead, he slept fitfully until daylight, when he woke, tired and sore. Looking around, he noticed, chillingly, that the bed and room were covered in plaster from the walls, seemingly torn off by the claws of the creature. Also, all the electrical cabling had been pulled from the walls. Of the creature, there was no sign.

Interestingly, a year after this encounter, Terry again came across the same strange creature, and once more, was simply too terrified to do anything. Whatever the

Mendips Beast was remains a complete mystery, although students visiting the building on overnight stays have been known to wedge chairs against the doors at night, just in case the bristly creature decides to return.

Interestingly, the Mendips have been the site of numerous big cat sightings in recent years, and savaged carcasses of sheep have been discovered, adding weight to claims that a giant alien big cat may be living in the area. Having said that, the ex-Royal Marine is adamant that what he encountered was no cat—and, indeed, no animal he could even imagine.

But if supernatural badger-like creatures are strange—indeed, almost inconceivable—our next fantastic story straddles the shadowy gap between the paranormal and the normal even more so. In point of fact, I hesitated on a number of occasions before including it in this book.

Sitting quietly in the picturesque, late eighteenth-century streetscape of Berkeley Square in the prestigious London suburb of Mayfair is a fairly nondescript four-storey brick house that, these days, holds the offices of an antiquarian bookseller. To passersby the house is nothing special, although it is smart and reflects an important part of London's long architectural history. And yet, behind this façade of normality is one of the most well-known and interesting cryptozoological/ ghost stories to ever come out of the United Kingdom.

The house at 50 Berkeley Square was once the home of George Canning, who served briefly as Prime Minister in 1827. At one stage, the house had also been the property of Marcus Samuel, First Viscount Bearsted, founder of the Shell Transport and Trading Company. It was also believed that, at one point in time, it was the oldest unaltered building in London.

However, fascinating as this is, it is not what we are interested in, as this quaint little place was once regarded as being the most haunted house in London. Ghosts aside, the case also seems to straddle the supernatural/cryptozoological world, with some claiming that the place was once haunted by some sort of undiscovered semi-aquatic, predatory cryptid.

When it comes to the subject of ghosts, I would suggest reading some of my other works on the subject, suffice to say that some suggest that the attic room is haunted by a spirit of a young woman who committed suicide by throwing herself from a top floor window after being abused by her uncle. Her spirit is said to take the form of a brown mist, although sometimes she is reported as being a white figure. She is also said to be capable of frightening people to death. Another legend, however, suggests that the ghost is that of a young man who was locked in the attic room and fed only through a hole in the door until he went mad and died.

Whatever the case, after Canning moved out the house was bought by a Mr Myers in 1885. Jilted by a previous lover, Myers would lock himself in the attic room—something that, over time, led to complete madness and eventual death. During this time the house became somewhat dilapidated, and its reputation as being haunted grew.

In 1872, Lord Lyttleton, a British aristocrat and Conservative politician, stayed a night in the building's attic for a bet. Knowing the reputation of the place, he brought his shotgun with him. Sometime during the night, he reported that an apparition appeared and, frightened, he shot at it. In the morning, however, all he could find were the spent shells of his shotgun. Whatever it was that he had shot at was gone.

In 1879, it was reported that a maid who had stayed in the attic room went completely mad and later died in an asylum. However, it was an event, reportedly in 1884, that really cemented the supernatural reputation of the house: Sir Robert Warboys, a nobleman, decided to take up a challenge of staying in the allegedly haunted room.

Warboys heard of the haunting while drinking at a tavern in the Holbrook district. Apparently hotheaded and very single-minded, he was dismissive of the legend and soon he found himself disagreeing with his drinking companions, Lord Cholmondley and John Benson (the owner of the house), who challenged him to spend a night in the haunted room.

Supremely confident, Warboys agreed to the bet, and proceeded to the haunted house, where he managed to convince the reluctant landlord to allow him to spend a night in the haunted room. However, before the landlord would allow him to do so, he specified that Warboys must be armed with a pistol and, at the first sign of anything strange, must pull a cord that was attached to a bell in the landlord's room below, as a warning sign. Warboys ridiculed the notion, but agreed to the terms.

According to the landlord, the spectre was a 'man-ghost' with a face that was "white and flabby with a huge gaping mouth, black as pitch". However, others said that it was an animal-like creature with many legs and tentacles, and that it could have crawled out of the London sewers. Whatever the case, it was agreed by all that, whatever it was, it was evil.

Warboys soon entered the haunted room where he closed the door and waited. The room was large and comfortably furnished with a double bed and armchairs. Two big windows overlooked the Square and a fire was burning in the hearth. Warboys, not expecting to sleep the night, lay on the bed, apparently propped up by pillows. At his side he had a cocked and loaded pistol.

At midnight the clock chimed, and the landlord assumed that everything was all right. However, sometime after midnight, he was awoken by the urgent clanging of the bell from the haunted room. Leaping out of bed to investigate, he heard a single gunshot and then silence.

Panting from a lack of breath after running up the stairs, the landlord opened the door. Warboys, previously sitting at the table when the landlord left him, was dead—his body cowered in the corner of the room, the still-smoking pistol in his white knuckles. For all intents and purposes, it appeared as if he had died of fright. Intriguingly, there were no signs of a struggle.

It was reported that Warboys's lips were peeled back from his clenched teeth in a grimace of horror, and his eyes appeared to be literally bulging from his skull. In the wall opposite the body, the landlord found a single bullet hole but nothing else. Whatever Warboys had fired at had not only scared him to death but had also disappeared into thin air. Later, a coroner pronounced that he had, in fact, died of fright; he was literally scared to death.

But this was not the only eerie death in the house as, only three years after death of Sir Robert Warboys, the house became the site of another grisly and unexplainable death. And, although the story varies in minor detail, the major premise of the story remains the same.

In 1887, two sailors from HMS *Penelope*, Robert Martin and Edward Blunden, wasted their money on a night of drunken celebration at being on shore. Short of money and a place to stay for the night, noticed a 'To Let' sign on the then abandoned Berkeley Square house. As it was late and no one was around, they broke into a basement window in search of somewhere to sleep for the night. The lower level of the house, however, was damp and rat-infested, so they headed upstairs, finally deciding to settle in the haunted room.

According to legend, sometime after midnight Blunden awoke when he heard the door to the room creak. Slowly, the door opened and a dim sliver of grey light began to creep across the wooden floor. Blunden was frozen in fear but managed to wake his shipmate, and the two men sat on the floor, listening as a strange, moist, scraping sound slowly approached them. Martin was later to claim that it sounded as if something was being dragged across the floor—or worse, that something was dragging *itself* across the floor.

Details are vague, but it appears that the two men managed to snap out of their fear-induced paralysis and came face to face with the creature, whatever it was, which blocked their only avenue of escape: the door. Blunden reached for his rifle, but the creature lunged at him and wrapped itself around his neck.

Panic-stricken, Martin seized the opportunity to escape and ran from the house screaming for help. A passing policeman soon heard his screams and, although sceptical of the tale, decided to follow him back to the house to ascertain what was going on. According to the sketchy accounts, Martin and the officer ran up the stairs but found no sign of Blunden in the room. Martin grabbed the rifle, and the two men searched the house for the missing man. However, there was no sign of him until they entered the damp, rat-infested basement where they found the dismembered corpse of the sailor. His body reportedly lay in a bloody heap, with his head wrenched violently to the side. The officer reported that the Blunden's eyes, similar to those of Warboys's three years previously, were wide open as if they had witnessed some unimaginable horror.

Although the story has been reported in many different guises over the years—indeed, even the dates are now somewhat debatable—it is thought that the creature/ghost was a shadowy man-like figure with a deformed face and body. Another discrepancy in the legend is that Blunden did not perish in the basement but was impaled on a spike on a wrought-iron fence that surrounded the house, suggesting that he had been thrown out of the window.

However, ghost or not, what interests us is that the creature has been described as an amorphous being, formless and slimy, and making a gruesome, sloppy, sliding noise when it moves. Others have suggested that it was a dark, shapeless, spectral form that attacked its victims with clawed feet and sharp, bird-like talons. Yet others have described it as a ghostly mist-like form that moves silently across the room towards its intended victim. Oddly enough, and more in line with the subject of this book, there is a school of thought that it had tentacles and was somewhat similar to an octopus.

Bizarrely, the 'octopus theory', as unlikely as it is, has led some paranormal and cryptozoological researchers to suggest that the creature may actually have been some kind of mutated freshwater octopus, or at least an unknown, amphibious, marine animal that had somehow managed to migrate from the Thames into London's vast subterranean sewer system and from there managed to enter the house at 50 Berkeley Square.

However, as previously mentioned, the house is now the premises of an antique bookshop, and if one is to believe local reports, nothing supernatural or paranormal has recently happened. At least, that is as much as we know—for, as we have seen with the strange Liverpool sewer creature that was reported in the *Liverpool Echo* in April 2011, such things may not be as unbelievable as we first thought.

Chapter Seven

Final Thoughts

In this book we have looked at a range of strange creatures that, quite inexplicably, keep popping up all over the British Isles. From mermaids on windswept rocky shores to lake monsters and Bigfoot-like creatures, we have seen that ordinary people keep experiencing bizarre, and sometimes quite frightening, creatures that either could not, or should not, exist.

Are all these people misguided? Have they, like Tom Adler and his vampire encounter, simply misinterpreted what he saw that dark night in the 1970s? Maybe it was steam, escaping from a vent? Or perhaps a patch of mist or fog? Or perhaps Adler witnessed something we can never hope to understand or explain?

Likewise, Martin Whitley, who photographed the infamous Beast of Dartmoor, and who was adamant it was not a wild dog. Is it simply a large hairy boar that, due to a trick of light, appears to be something other than a pig? Or is it possible that something unknown is roaming the lonely tors and craggy hilltops of Dartmoor?

Of course, I could have added other mythological creatures such as the *Bean Nighe*, a figure in Scottish folklore that is said to foretell the deaths of mortals, and appears as a washerwoman who cleans the bloody clothes of those who are fated to die. Or the *Dearg-Due*, once a beautiful woman, who killed herself in order to avoid an arranged marriage after falling in love with a peasant boy, and who later rose from the grave and killed her family for forcing her into such a miserable state.

Other interesting and relevant creatures such as the *Dobhar-chú*, or 'water hound', could have been studied. This legendary otter-like animal reputedly lives in isolated freshwater lakes and rivers in Ireland, and has been described as being a half-dog, half-fish hybrid with a long, snaking body covered in thick fur. And while it is highly improbable that it exists, it could simply be a huge otter.

And while on the subject of overly large animals, we should quickly examine the phenomenon of huge rabbits and hares, often reported being seen in the countryside. Hares are among the most delightful of British animals and through history have been held up as symbols of fertility and Easter. They are often attributed with supernatural or magical powers but are in no way aggressive or menacing to humans. Having said that, a number of eyewitness accounts have suggested that sometimes these enigmatic creatures can grow to extreme sizes.

Recently, in Banbury in Oxfordshire, a number of extraordinary sightings of a gigantic rabbit were reported. The first of these took place one early evening during summer 2005, when Clive Parker was driving home to Wendlebury, just twenty miles south of Banbury, when he observed what he considered to be a gigantic rabbit squatting at the roadside. He estimated it to be as big as a large dog, light brown in colour, with a somewhat pointed face, and sitting on its haunches, watching him as he drove past. It took him a few moments to register what he'd seen, but by the time he had turned his car around and drove back for another look, the huge rabbit was gone.

Another sighting, this time with multiple witnesses, took place on 24 October 2006 when Tim Hill, his family, and some friends were travelling along the Napton–Banbury canal on a narrowboat. At one stage of the journey, they looked to their right across a sloping field and saw what they thought at first to be a deer, although roughly the size of a golden retriever dog. When Hill's wife, Mandy, and one of their friends, David, looked at it through binoculars they were astonished to realise that it was, in fact, a giant rabbit. It then hopped away under a hedgerow and was never seen again.

Interestingly, in early April 2006, a similar mystery animal was causing consternation for gardeners who worked allotments on public ground in Felton. The gardeners complained that their vegetables were being frequently trampled upon and eaten each night by a dog-sized rabbit which that behind giant-sized footprints. As this encounter took place not long after the cinema release of the Wallace and Gromit film, *The Curse of the Were-Rabbit*, a high degree of scepticism was justified— and yet, the gardeners still protested that it was real.

Then, on 11 May, Rael Rawlinson, an eighteen-year-old student, revealed that a month earlier she had been driving along a road near Felton when she collided with and killed a "massive, abnormally big" rabbit that measured over two feet in length.

But abnormally large rabbits are not really that impressive when we are speaking of cryptozoological anomalies. However, some gargantuan creatures are worthy of note. For instance, at Inglewood Pond in Clackmannanshire, what was described as a horse-dog was seen on two separate occasions, firstly in 1975 by two women, then in 1997, where a witness reported seeing a strange horse with the legs of a dog cavorting around the woods in broad daylight before vanishing into the woods.

Equally puzzling is the following, which happened in the Nursery Woods in Cumbria in January 2006 when a person reported seeing a large pterosaur-like creature flying above the woods. Is this perhaps what Sally Chapman and others reported seeing the Mawnan, Cornwall, in the mid-1970s? Surely not, as the distance between the two places in near to six hundred kilometres, and even for a man-sized bird this would be some feat of endurance. Having said that, many birds *do* fly thousands of kilometres each year—so maybe, just maybe, the Owlman and the strange pterosaur could have been one and the same?

But pterosaurs are not the only apparently extinct creatures that keep getting regularly reported. As we have seen, reports of loch and lake monsters are, if not common, are certainly not unusual. Indeed, apart from my experience with a seal in Inverness, I also witnessed a number of strange hump-like shapes in Loch Ness when I was there in the summer of 2015. Were these sightings evidence of the enigmatic and secretive Nessie? I think not. In fact, they were probably the wake of a boat that had passed minutes before, because the loch, being so deep and narrow, forms strange hump-like waves in certain circumstances. Could it be that all sightings of the Loch Ness Monster are nothing more than misidentified waves? Looking at the evidence, one would have to conclude in the negative. How else could someone describe, as did George Spicer in July 1933, "a most extraordinary form of animal" shuffling across the road in front of their car? An animal described as described having a large body, about four feet high and twenty-five feet long, with a long, narrow neck, slightly thicker than an elephant's trunk?

Equally, what of GE Taylor, the South African tourist who, in 1938, managed to take three minutes of film of something in the loch? And Tim Dinsdale, whose 1960 film still has people scratching their heads?

And even more fascinating is that we see almost identical reports coming from Loch Morar, where the crystal-clear waters are supposed to hide another beast, Morag, described by John MacVarish in August 1968 as having "a snake-like head, very small compared to the size of the neck—flattish, a flat type of head. It was very dark, nearly black. It looked as if it was paddling itself along."

Adrian Shine, the leader of the Loch Ness Project, has scoured the waters of both lochs for decades and remains highly sceptical, suggesting that the legend is based more upon the nature of human perception and myth-making than a real animal. And yet, even he acknowledges that such monsters *could* exist—maybe not in the loch itself, but elsewhere in the world: "The deep sea has possibilities. It's hard to imagine any other environments. But it does rely to a degree on a Lost World. See, the Himalayas are very remote, and the forests of North America are more remote than you might think—there is a lot of it—but of course Bigfoot is less credible. And water is a hostile environment. You know the Lost World of Conan Doyle exists on a plateau, an isolated plateau. You have got the Congo, you have got the Nile, you have got Lost Worlds, but the big Lost World at the moment is the deep ocean, which we have only scratched."

But lake and river monsters aside, surely reports of vampiric activity can only be put down to folklore stories and a morbid fascination with death. After all, Whitby in North Yorkshire was the setting for the most famous vampire novel of all time and is now the so-called capital of the world for the 'Goth' subculture, whose imagery and cultural proclivities indicate influences from the nineteenth-century Gothic literature along with horror films.

And yet one gets the feeling that *something* strange is happening, and although David Farrant—who once believed that the Highgate vampire could exist within the walls of Highgate Cemetery—now tends to discount the vampire theory and instead blames it upon a fascination with horror films and a mild hysteria, reports of the tall black figure have not ceased, with the most recent at Highgate Cemetery being in 2005.

And even if we are to take into account Bram Stoker's *Dracula*, then what are we to make of the incredibly strange tale of the vampire if Croglin Grove, which, although published in the 1920s, could have been based on a story from the late 1600s—which means that it could not have been influenced by Stoker's book in any way. And yet, even if we concede that vampires are more legend and myth than flesh and blood, we still cannot quite remove the thought, however slight it may be, that such creatures may exist, even if not in the traditional sense. This has been demonstrated by the story of Sarah Donald, in the early 1980s in Leith, who was apparently attacked by something similar to a vampire. Is it possible that Donald was mistaken and that, in fact, she had encountered something even more nefarious: the medieval monster of nightmares, the Incubus, the male form of demon that lies upon women in order to engage in sexual activity with them and, over time, drains their life force?

Who can say? And yet, as the Reverend Lionel Fanthorpe noted, over the past hundred years, Britain has recorded over two hundred stories about vampires, and that there are around two alleged sightings per year.

But if vampires are more the stuff of legend and myth than actual entities, what can we make of reports of large, hairy men running around the woods and glens of the British Isles? Surely Bigfoot or his English equivalent could not exist? However, once again we are confronted with numerous eyewitness accounts of just such creatures. From Caroline Toms's sighting in Sussex in November of 2005, to the 'Kentish Apeman', who has been regularly seen around Tunbridge Wells, to the extremely weird Cannock Chase in central England, where reports of big cats, black dogs, Bigfoot-like creatures, and werewolves are not unusual.

And what of stories of werewolves and other strange creatures that seem to lurk in the dark woods of Cannock Chase? How can so many reports of strange phenomena come from one specific area? And by so many people—regular, normal, and apparently sane people? Can they all be suffering from delusions, or are they simply misinterpreting what they have seen, given that the night, shadows, and environmental conditions (such as fog and mist) distort our perception and challenge our established views?

Or is it simply suggestion? Is it possible that these people have read something, or seen a television programme, and a seed has been planted in their minds? A seed that somehow tricks the brain into seeing not what is there but what we expect to find? Is this the case with 'Old Stinker', who is said to haunt the Yorkshire Wolds? But then, how could one mistake a huge half-man, half-wolf-like creature that can effortlessly leap over thirty feet in a single bound while holding a dog in its mouth? Surely suggestion cannot explain this?

As for Gef (the supposed talking mongoose) and Spring-heeled Jack, as well as other creatures and entities that seem beyond belief, I shall leave it up to the mind of the reader to decide whether they exist or not. And really, this is so for most of these creatures—although, one must agree, at times there does appear to be a speck of truth in the witness sightings. After all, can all these people be so wrong? Can they all have misinterpreted what they have seen? Without doubt, these onlookers have witnessed something strange, something outside the bounds of what we consider normal.

It seems to me that the British not only love but also warmly embrace the possibility that exotic and sometimes dangerous animals might be lurking around in the otherwise picturesque woods, valleys, lakes, and hillsides. Is this because, over the centuries, real wild animals such as wolves and bears have been wiped out and somehow there remains as residual memory or yearning for these more dangerous, and therefore more glamorous, times? Do we as humans still yearn to be seen as brave conquerors of the wild woods? Are we masters of our destiny, longing for a nostalgic but unreal life where we eke out a life in a savage and unforgiving landscape, when, in fact, we wake in our heated, safe houses, drive to work, before buying our food at a supermarket? In Britain, the most dangerous thing you will probably come across is an enraged bull—and this certainly doesn't fit the bill of a dangerous, exotic animal. Whatever the case, over the last few years, there have also been stories about a giant goose-eating fish in the London Olympic Park, another lion in Gloucestershire, as well as wolves on Dartmoor.

To be fair, in the past, strange animals have occasionally turned up and, indeed, defied identification. In 1810, a brown, striped, dog-sized predator with huge jaws killed over three hundred sheep in northwest England. Dubbed the 'Vampire dog of Ennerdale', it was so elusive and destructive that some locals believed it was a werewolf. Local sheepdogs dared not attack it, and for six months hunters could not catch it. Today, it's thought that the creature was nothing more than a Tasmanian tiger (*Thylacinus cynocephaluse*) that had escaped from a zoo or travelling menagerie.

As well, Police Constable Bishop's strange encounter in April 1954 in Ramsgate, Kent, with a so-called 'walking fir cone' appears to be either a pangolin or a shingleback skink. Of course, it is also possibly that it was something else, something completely unknown to man.

Recent reports have indicated that wallabies, and even a kangaroo, have been sighted in various parts of England, which suggests that people, although prone to misidentification, also tend to get things right. This probably explains why, when Richard the Lionheart's pet crocodile escaped from the Royal Menagerie in the Tower of London and swam down to the North Essex marshes, locals reported seeing a dragon!

As such, is it possible that escaped crocodiles of today are what dragons were to our forebears? Did they simply not know what they were seeing and therefore described the creature in a way they knew and understood?

But this, of course, raises the question: what *was* it that staff at the North West Water Company United Utilities saw on their closed-circuit cameras in the sewers beneath the streets of Liverpool? Surely such a hideous humanoid creature cannot exist? And yet, the evidence suggests that it does—whatever *it* is. Equally, what sort of creature harassed and terrified a sane, logical and no-

nonsense ex-Royal Marine in a lonely building in the wilds of the Mendips? Was it simply a curious badger or something else, something unknown to science—indeed, something seemingly paranormal, as if not of this world?

Interestingly, for some reason humans have what appears to be an inbuilt urge to believe in peculiar and unusual creatures. When we hear there might be something odd lurking nearby, we are fascinated, if not a little afraid—probably an evolutionary trait from hundreds of thousands of years ago, when we were simply small apes living in a dangerous African landscape and where pretty much everything was monstrous and dangerous. To put it simply: we like to believe in monsters, even when there's little evidence to attest to their existence.

Dr Karl Shuker, a zoologist who specialises in unexplained phenomena and creatures, suggests: "The likelihood, however remote, of encountering one of these creatures provides a frisson of suppressed primeval fear that can still be expressed or released just by reading about them."

Of course, there could be other explanations. After all, how can so many people report seeing so many strange creatures the length and breadth of the countryside? As we have seen with the so-called Bristol crocodile, strange and exotic animals can survive in unfamiliar climates. As for the others—the black dogs, the loch monsters, the wild, hairy men, and even vampires–well, that is for the reader to decide.

Reference List and Further Reading

Arment, C. (2004) *Cryptozoology: Science & Speculation*. Coachwhip Publications.

Arnold, N. (2010) *Paranormal Kent*. The History Press: Gloucestershire.

Andrews, C. (2014) 'From mystery beasts to big cats, England's wilder than you think', *Earth Touch News Network*, 3 April.

Bagot, M. (2014) 'Is this the Loch Ness Monster? Creature photographed in lake—150 miles from home', *The Mirror*, 11 September.

Bayless, R. (1970) *Animal Ghosts*. University Books: New York.

'Beware the Welsh Teggie, witches and more' (2006) *Wales Online*, 27 February.

'Bigfoot "sighting" in Hopwas Woods by Tamworth man?' (2015) *Tamworth Herald*, 7 February.

Bord, J. (1997) *Fairies: Real Encounters with Little People*. Michael O'Mara: London.

Bord, J., & Bord, C. (1985) *Alien Animals*. Panther Books: London.

'Bow-nessie takes a bow' (2007) *Northern Echo*, 23 February.

Brown, A. (2015) 'The new Nessie? First photos of 20ft crocodile lurking off British coast', *The Express*, 9 February.

Branagan, M. (2016) 'Residents trembling in terror after seeing "8 FOOT WEREWOLF" in British city', *The Express,* 15 May.

Camber, R. (2007) 'Demon of Dartmoor: mystery beast seen at hell hound's haunt', *Daily Mail*, 29 July.

Campbell, S. (2002) *The Loch Ness Monster: The Evidence.* Birlinn Limited: Edinburgh.

'The Celtic folklore traditions of Halloween' (2015) Interview with Dr Jenny Butler. *Transceltic*, 11 October 2015 (originally published in October 2013).

Chamberlain, T. (2006) 'Photo in the News: Loch Ness Monster Was an Elephant?', *National Geographic*, 9 March.

Christian, C. (2015) *A travel guide to Yorkshire's Weird Wolds: The Mysterious Wold Newton Triangle*.

Coleman, L. & Huyghe, P. (2003) *A Field Guide to Lake Monsters, Sea Serpents and Other Mystery Denizens of the Deep.* Penguin Group: New York.

Congdon, J. (2015) 'Seven animal sightings which have never been explained', *The Express*, 24 March.

Cramb, A. (2008) 'DNA could help identify 200-year-old Stronsay Beast', *The Telegraph*, 3 September.

Daniels, C. (2012) 'Britain's Bigfoot spotted in Tunbridge Wells', *Kent News*, 20 November.

Dinsdale, T. (1961) *Loch Ness Monster*. Routledge & Kegan Paul: London.

Dixon, C. (2012) 'Are we still away with the fairies?', *Irish Examiner*, 21 December.

Downes, J. (2001) *The Owlman and Others*. CFZ Communications.

Eberhart, G.M. (2002) *Mysterious Creatures: A Guide to Cryptozoology*. Santa Barbara.

English, R. (2009) 'Croydon Tinker Bell... are there fairies at the bottom of the garden?', *Daily Mail,* 8 September.

'The faeries of the Cornish tin mines—Cousin Jack and the TommyKnockers' (2014), *Transceltic*, 1 September.

Fairley, J. & Welfare, S. (1982) *Arthur C Clarke's Mysterious World*.

Finan, V. (2016) 'Has the Loch Ness Monster moved to London? Mysterious footage captures unknown creature swimming in the Thames', *Daily Mail*, 6 April.

'Ghost sightings highest in 25 years' (2010) *The Telegraph*, 26 April.

Graham, C. (2016) 'Has Loch Ness Monster moved to the Thames?', *The Telegraph*, 6 April.

Guiley, R.E. (2005) *The Encyclopedia of Vampires, Werewolves, and Other Monsters*. Facts On File, Inc: New York.

Hacker, S. (2002) 'Days out: the shy monster of Bala lake', *The Independent*, 24 February.

Halliday, R. (2010) *Edinburgh After Dark: Vampires, Ghosts and Witches of the Old Town*. Black and White Publishing: Edinburgh.

Hardy, J. (2015) 'Is the Bristol crocodile back? Witness said "croc winked at me" after sighting in river', *The Mirror,* 10 July.

Harris, P. (2009) 'Is this the Beast of Exmoor? Body of mystery animal washes up on beach', *Daily Mail*, 9 January.

—— (2011) 'Is this Bownessie? Four-humped beastie spotted in Lake Windermere', *Daily Mail*, 21 February.

—— (2014) 'Is this the skeleton of legendary devil dog Black Shuck who terrorised 16th century East Anglia?', *Daily Mail*, 16 May.

Harrison, P. (1999) *The Encyclopaedia of the Loch Ness Monster*. Robert Hale: London.

—— (2002) *Sea Serpents and Lake Monsters of the British Isles*. Robert Hale: London.

Heuvelmans, B. (1968) *In the Wake of the Sea-Serpents*. Hill and Wang.

—— (1995) *On the Track of Unknown Animals*. Kegan Paul International Ltd.

Howell, H. (2016) 'Scottish Vampire Legends', published 18 April.

'Hunt is on for the Beast of Badcox' (2006) *Frome & Somerset Standard*, 7 September.

'Is Bigfoot in Britain? Mysterious figure lurking in Lincolnshire woods is claimed to be mystery beast' (2014) *The Mirror*, 2 December.

Killarney, A.L. (2003) 'Monster "fish" in Killarney lake think scientists', *Irish Times*, 18 August.

Kirkpatrick B. (2005) *Nessie: The Legend of the Loch Ness Monster*. Crombie Jardine Publishing Limited: Edinburgh.

'Loch Morar monster Morag sightings uncovered' (2013), *BBC News,* 25 February.

Mackal, R.P. (1980) *Searching for Hidden Animals.* Doubleday.

Mackinley, J. (1893) *Folklore of Scottish Lochs and Springs.* William Hodge & Co: Glasgow.

Mann, S. (2016) 'River Thames Monster: Fresh sightings fuel speculation of creature lurking in the depths', *Evening Standard*, 11 April.

Matthews, R. (2010) *Strange Animals.* Unexplained. Quarto group Company: London.

McCann, J. (2014) 'Forget the tales, fairies are back and with an attitude', *The Express*, 14 December.

McEwan, G.J. (1986) *Mystery Animals of Britain and Ireland.* Robert Hale: London.

McKillop, J. (1998) *Dictionary of Celtic Mythology.* Oxford University Press: New York.

McPhee, R. (2013) 'Top 10 British mysteries, spectres, unexplained deaths, and alien encounters', *The Mirror*, 20 November.

—— (2014) 'Vampire Britain: UK could be home to more blood-sucking nightfeeders than Dracula's homeland', *The Mirror*, 16 September.

Meredith, C. (2013) 'Legend of Loch Ness to be overshadowed as new monster mystery is unearthed', *The Express*, 26 February.

'Merseyside sewer monster hunt, after mysterious beast seen on CCTV' (2013) *Liverpool Echo*, 7 May.

Miles, C. (1908) 'Experiments in thought transference', *Journal of the Society for Psychical Research*.

Monaghan, P. (2008) *The Encyclopedia of Celtic Mythology and Folklore*. Checkmark Books.

Montgomery, J.G. (2014) *WYRD—A journey into the beliefs and philosophies of the known and unknown*. CFZ Publications: Devon.

—— (2012) *A Case for Ghosts*. Ginninderra Press: Adelaide.

'Mystery beasts spotted all over Scotland' (2014) *Scotland Now*, 21 November.

'Mystery "beast" spotted roaming Plymouth suburbs' (2016) *The Telegraph*, 7 April.

'Mystery big cat spotted' (2010) *Whitehaven News* (website), 28 July.

O'Neill, K. (2014) 'Seven terrifying mystery beasts that never existed: from real-life Gollum to Owl Man of Cornwall', *The Mirror*, 15 December.

'Panther and puma at large' (2004) *BBC News,* 24 September.

Proctor, K. (2011) '"Bownessie" spotted again by holidaymakers', *Westmorland Gazette,* 24 February.

Purtill, C. (2014) 'This Irish cottage may be haunted by violent fairies', *USA Today*, 22 November.

Puttick, B. (Ed) (2002) *Supernatural England.* Countryside Books: Newbury, Berkshire.

Radford, B. & Nichell. J (2006) *Lake Monster Mysteries: Investigating the World's Most Elusive Creatures*. University Press of Kentucky.

Redfern, N. (2006) 'The werewolves of Britain', *FATE magazine*, March.

Reilly, J. (2014) 'Away with the fairies? University lecturer claims to have photographed real-life tiny Tinkerbells flying through the air in the British countryside', *Daily Mail*, 4 April.

Roberts, G. (2014) 'Beast of Bodmin Moor: mystery solved over "beast" that slaughtered farm animals for decades', *The Mirror*, 15 December.

Sherman, A. (2014) *Vampires: The Myths, Legends and Lore*. Adams Media: Avon, MA.

Shuker, K.P.N. (2009) *The Unexplained: An Illustrated Guide to the World's Paranormal Mysteries*. Sterling.

Siddique, H. (2016) 'Loch Ness Monster: remains of film model discovered by robot', *The Guardian*, 13 April.

Sieveking, P. (2005) 'A field guide to the mystery beasts of the British Isles', *The Independent*, 26 March.

Smith, O. (2015) 'Terrifying "Roch Ness Monster" found washed up by British lake', *The Express*, 4 August.

'Snaps heighten speculation on creature in lake' (2009), *Express & Echo*, 28 September.

Snelling, D. (2014) 'Has even the Loch Ness Monster left Scotland? Mysterious creature snapped in ENGLISH lake', *The Express*, 12 September.

Spicer, K. (2014) 'Vampire Island: Britain is a bloodsucking hotspot', *International Business Times*, 17 September.

Stanley, T. (2015) 'Return of the fairy-hunters', *The Spectator*, 3 January.

Steiger, B. (2011) *Real Monsters, Gruesome Critters and Beasts from the Darkside*. Visible Ink Press: Canton, MI.

Strachan, G. (2015a) '"My reports of seeing a monster were not taken seriously" woman says she saw Bigfoot in Angus', *The Courier*, 22 January.

—— (2015b) 'I've experienced some crazy stuff but this was a big surprise' former civil servant tells of night he saw Bigfoot in Fife', *The Courier*, 30 January.

Taylor, M. (2009) 'Swimmer hit by "monster" wake', *Westmorland Gazette*, 23 July.

Tim the Yowie Man (2001) *The Adventures of Tim the Yowie-Man*. Random House: Milson's Point.

Vale, P. (2015) '"British Bigfoot" spotted by border collie on forest walk in Sussex, dog owner takes a photograph', *Huffington Post*, 9 November.

Ware, J. (2016) 'The werewolf of Hull! Witnesses claim they've spotted 8ft tall fanged beast with human-like features nicknamed "Old Stinker"', *Daily Mail*, 15 May.

Winter, S. (2010) 'Hunt for the huge Black Dogs haunting UK's countryside', *The Express*, 4 July.

Young, S. (2015) Interview in *The Big Issue*, 22 January.

Weblinks

http://anomalyinfo.com
http://cryptomundo.com
http://cryptosightings.com
http://cryptozoo-oscity.blogspot.com.au
http://forteanzoology.blogspot.com.au
http://hayleyisaghost.co.uk
http://karlshuker.blogspot.com.au
http://realunexplainedmysteries.com
http://santinibasra.com/Adrian-Shine
http://www.earthtouchnews.com
http://www.mysteriousbritain.co.uk
http://www.orkneyjar.com
http://www.paranormaldatabase.com
http://www.phantomsandmonsters.com
http://www.scapaflow.co
http://www.simonsherwood.co.uk
http://www.spookyisles.com
http://www.strangemag.com
http://www.transceltic.com
http://www.unofficialbritain.com
https://lindagodfrey.com
http://www.wildaboutbritain.co.uk

Every effort has been made to ensure all source material is listed. However, it is possible that I have missed some references and if this is so, then I apologise to the original author or publication.

See also: www.jgmontgomeryauthor.com

About The Author

JG Montgomery is an Australian/ English writer. He is a former Rural Fire Service and Emergency Services training officer. He was born in Cornwall in the United Kingdom, the son of an Australian Air Force officer.

He is a bass player, guitarist, vocalist and songwriter in a 70s-style rock band and has released four full-length albums with a previous band plus a solo album in 2018.

He previously served in both the Australian Army Reserve and Australian Air Force. He has university degrees in cultural heritage and teaching, a diploma in Parapsychology and was once a cricket coach. He is also a decorated State Emergency Service volunteer having been awarded a distinguished service medal in the 2021 Queen's Birthday Honours.

White Horse Dreaming is his tenth book to date.

He lives in Canberra, Australia, with his partner Kirsten, two cats, a short black dog, some ducks and chickens and a lot of goldfish.

www.blossomspringpublishing.com